Bar-Track Man

Gerald B. Garner

PublishAmerica
Baltimore

First printing

ISBN: 1-4137-4198-3 (softcover)
ISBN: 978-1-4489-7795-6 (hardcover)
PUBLISHED BY PUBLISHAMERICA, LLLP
www.publishamerica.com
Baltimore

Printed in the United States of America

Dedication

This book is dedicated to my lady, my soul-mate, my wife.

To Sue
Gerald B. Garner

Acknowledgments

Excerpts were taken from the following publications:

The book *Earthfire*, written by C. Rosenfeld and R. Cooke, published by M.I.T. Press in 1982. The book *Predicting Volcanic Eruptions* written by G. Vogt and published by Franklin Watts in 1989.

Author's Notes

Mt. St. Helens, the Cascade Range volcanoes and the volcanoes in Mexico and Central America are elements of the so called RING OF FIRE. It extends down through South America, around to New Zealand, up to Japan, and over through the Aleutian Islands and Alaska. This ring bordering the Pacific Ocean floor stands as the most violent active zone of seismic and volcanic tumult in the world.

This RING OF FIRE is a sign the sea floor is splitting along a jagged seam. On both sides of this seam the massive crustal plates are slowly pulling away from each other, being shoved laterally toward land, the continents.

Along the RING OF FIRE there is great heat and volcanic underwater activity. This is visible from outer space and is watched and photographed by astronauts.

As the sliding of these crustal plates occur collisions are, of course, inevitable. When sea floor slabs crunch up against other slabs such as the American plate (the plate off the west coast of the United States) something must give. Since sea floor plates are denser and heavier basaltic material they cause the lighter continental plates to ride up, overlapping the oceanic plates.

This creates a so-called subduction zone. Theory holds that this descending material reaches depths of 200 miles or 300 kilometers, and is melted by the earth's interior heat and the massive friction being created. This molten material is under great pressure and seeks a way out through cracks and fissures toward earth's surface.

Thus, you have volcanic activity from a slow process. What would happen if this process was rapidly speeded up by simultaneous volcanic eruptions along the RING OF FIRE forcing the plates of oceanic material to move much faster?

A chain reaction resulting in massive earthquake and volcanic activity worldwide. An end to modern life as predicted at a meeting of scientists in San Francisco, California on December 7, 1993.

Preface

LOS ANGELES TIMES, DECEMBER 7, 1993 PUBLICATION

On Tuesday, December 7, 1993, during a meeting of U.S. and European scientists in San Francisco, California, a warning was issued that mammoth volcanic eruptions have been occurring somewhere in the world on an average of once every hundred years, and when the next one strikes it is likely to cause enormous disruption to modern life.

One of the best examples of how an eruption can change the world is the eruption of Mt. Tambora on the island of Sumbawa, two hundred miles south of Macassar and seven hundred and fifty miles east of Bolivia. The mountain self-destructed in the largest known eruption in historic time. This eruption started on April 5, 1815 and culminated on April 10 and 11 in a series of hellish explosions that shook the entire Indonesian Island chain. Thousands were killed in the explosions and tens of thousands perished afterwards from starvation and cholera.

This giant eruption altered the earth's climate for over a year. Scientists estimate the power of this eruption at 4,200 hydrogen bombs. The dust circled the globe. The volcanic gas produced long term cooling of the earth's atmosphere. In the New England states during June and July crop-killing frosts occurred. Then in August a hard frost destroyed all crops. In Europe crop losses were high. In France, people ate their work animals and their pets to survive. All this resulted from just one volcanic eruption.

October 2, 2010

Astronauts returning from a stay on an international space station are startled to see a widening glow along the RING OF FIRE in the Pacific ocean. They attempt to call Houston and Kennedy control centers to report their observations. They receive no answer. Houston is a smoldering ruin and Kennedy is under the sea. Communication, other than a few battery powered ham radios, no longer exists. Huge earthquakes followed by extensive volcanic activity have and continue to tear the surface of the earth apart. The end of modern mankind has come.

Few people are destined to survive. This is the story of one of the few.

Gerald B. Garner
4652 Prior Court,
Arden Hills, MN 55112

Chapter 1

I stood and studied the track for a long time. It was the first human track I had seen in over two years.

It was early November 2013 and I had hunted farther out from my cabin then I had in a long time. With the coming of another severe winter in the next few weeks, I didn't want to exhaust what little game there still was close in. The last two winters had taught me a bitter lesson.

With the constant ash and dust from the eruptions blocking the winter sun the last two winters, I figured the resulting prolonged bitter cold finished off most of the few humans that were still living. Winter seemed to arrive in early September and last until early June. Although little snow seemed to fall, the temperatures were 20 to 30 degrees below zero nearly every night. I knew few farm crops could have been grown the past two summers, and from what little information I had gotten very few people were left.

What few city people that had survived the first winter surely starved or died of cholera from drinking the water that went bad. All the cities had lost all water and power the first few days of the quakes. Then the dust and choking gases swept in from the endless eruptions. With no clean water, cholera spread through the cities. With no electrical power, people burned anything to get heat. But the end came for most when after a few short months the food ran out. I am sure the old, that could not provide for themselves died first. Then the women and children that had no fathers or fathers that had no skill or training on how to survive.

I think the farmers were the last to go. They would have had canned goods and their own clean water from their wells, and most importantly, their live-stock. But with the arrival of marauding bands of food hunters that would kill for any kind of food, the livestock were soon consumed and stored foods quickly devoured. Farmers that weren't killed were left to starve.

Only one kind of man could survive. A man with knowledge of the woods and the wildlife it held. A true survivalist.

As I looked down at the tracks in the slowly falling snow, a wary feeling rose within me. The memory returned of the roving bands of food thieves and killers walking the roads even in this remote area. They raided cabins and homes those first few months after the quakes and eruptions had started. But then as the quakes and eruptions continued the earth has split or risen or fell in so many places that travel even by foot was nearly impossible. In few places did one tenth of a straight mile of traversable road remain. I had seen few people since.

I crouched down to study the track and meditate on the situation. From what little snow that had accumulated in the tracks, whoever had made them was still within a few minutes of where I was. It probably was a man due to the size of the track and about my weight. I judged that from comparing the depth of his track in the snow compared with my own. But something was odd about his right boot print, it angled in at the toe. Also, there seemed to be a bar-like cross tread in the instep area of his boot. I thought maybe he was wearing a wrapping of some kind around the right boot.

I figured I was about two miles out from my cabin and it being only about noon, I decided I would follow and see if I could overtake the track maker. It took only a few minutes on his trail to realize he was moving very slowly and cautiously. Whenever he reached good cover he would turn to check his back trail. He must have had good reason to do so and this made me move with caution and the skill I'd developed to survive these past three years in the wilderness. I warily stayed with the tracks always checking ahead for signs of movement or anything that appeared out of place. He was headed due north and would pass about a mile east of my cabin. In about twenty minutes I figured he would hit what was left of a gravel road that ran east and west.

There was nothing but woods for over ten miles to the east until you hit a little town called Brimson. No one lived there anymore. I had been there about a year ago while out looking for supplies and found all the buildings abandoned. To the west the road ended at a blacktop road that ran from the town of Duluth to several towns to the north that were located on what was known as the Minnesota Iron Range. There was little left of that road due to many deep crevices left from the quakes and the shifting earth.

Then I caught sight of him just as he approached the road. I crouched in under the pines and watched him. He again stopped, turned and studied his back trail. Then he cautiously walked out onto the road. He looked to his left and right but I knew he couldn't see more then a few yards in either direction due to the encroaching vegetation. Luckily, I waited before I followed him because he reappeared. He had several pine boughs in his hands. He crossed the road toward me then walked backwards while brushing out his tracks with the pine boughs. When he reached the far side of the road, the rifle he was carrying strapped over his shoulder slipped down his arm, nearly hitting the gravel road. I could see his mouth moving and I'm sure he was cussing. I would have done the same thing if I had dropped my rifle. It doesn't take much of a bump to knock a scope out of adjustment and with game getting more scarce each day a missed shot meant hungry nights. He then slowly disappeared into the pines.

I contemplated following but it was obvious that he didn't want to be seen. So I turned and headed for my cabin. As I moved out to the west I had an ominous feeling I would run into the man who left the bar-track again. It was a bad feeling.

Reaching my cabin just before dark I thought better of lighting my wood stove to heat my supper. Wood smoke can be detected a long ways in the woods and I still had the man I had seen on my mind. So, I finished last nights venison cold. One thing about the nights being cold is I didn't have any problem keeping things from spoiling. After supper I lit my candle and made my daily entry in my journal. I had started it when I realized I was more or less forced to stay in my cabin after those quakes and eruptions did there best to destroy the world.

I had come up to my hunting cabin as I did every fall a few weeks before the opening of the deer hunting season. I chopped enough wood to keep the place warm for the three week season and checked the cabin for any needed repairs. I had brought along my chain saw and ax, some cooking utensils and my down sleeping bag. Little did I know I would not have survived what was about to come without those items. Also, as I usually did, I had brought my two deer rifles and my favorite handgun, a Browning Buckmark .22 automatic. The rifle I hunted with was a Winchester bolt action .270. I had owned that gun for years.

The other rifle was an old 30-30 Winchester that my granddad had given me many years back. It ejected shells out the top so it had a side mounted scope. I never hunted with it anymore but carried it up to the cabin as a backup in case I, or someone hunting with me, had a problem with their gun and needed one. It had come in handy more then once. The scope on my .270 was a 3 x 9 power. For the area I hunted it was more then I required. Due to the thick brush I kept it set on four and never moved it. A shot of more then eighty yards in this area was pretty rare.

A couple of other items that I had brought along that proved to be invaluable were my compass and a battery powered radio. After that first night of unbelievable quakes with the ground heaving and splitting, I knew there was no way I could ever drive out of where I was. Between that portable radio and my truck radio I managed to keep informed of the destruction and chaos that were occurring around the world. Finally the broadcasts tapered off, I guess due to the depletion of the broadcast station's battery power. For a while I did get some ham radio transmissions that told a grim story of masses of people that were starving and lawlessness in the cities and towns. Huge fires were burning in the cities and towns from underground gas pipes that were ruptured in thousands of places. Few buildings were standing, and with no clean water cholera was spreading quickly. Then, even the ham transmissions quit.

Chapter 2

I wiped down my rifle with an oil rag as I did daily and put it in the rack over my bunk. It was like a friend to me and luckily I had been able to find some shells for it while out checking cabins and the abandoned houses for things I could use to help me survive. There were only two loads that were sold in stores for the .270, either a 130 or 150 grain. I had some of both, but in the short distance I was shooting, it made little difference if a round flew an inch lower or higher.

I then started my nightly routine of sit-ups and push-ups. Keeping myself in good shape was essential for my survival. I stood an inch under six feet and went about 170 pounds. I was fifty years old but solid as a rock. Chopping holes through the ice on nearby Sullivan Lake and chopping lots of firewood kept my upper body hard. I had quit smoking years ago and never was much of a drinking man. I walked miles every day, except in bad weather, while hunting so my legs were in great shape. I had hunted and fished all my life and having grown up on a farm, I could butcher any game with expertise.

I washed up and went out to answer natures call before bedding down for the night. I checked the area and listened to the evening sounds. Everything appeared normal so I went in and crawled into my sleeping bag. My little cabin was twelve by twenty and had been built to sleep six on three double bunks. I had eliminated two of the double bunks but had left the bunk over my head for storage. I had a barrel stove for heat and that thing really ate the firewood. The chain saw I had brought along had long since ran out of gas. I had siphoned the gas out of my pickup and mixed it with a little engine oil but the saw had eaten that up too. Thank God I had my ax, although I had found several in the cabins I had searched looking for things I could use.

The woods around the cabin consisted of birch and norway pine with a few cedars in the low areas. Firewood was about the only thing I had a good supply of. Besides chopping wood, I used those axes to chop holes in the nearby lake in the winter. Supplementing my diet with some sunfish and an occasional crappie was a lot better then venison and rabbit every night.

I finally dozed off knowing I would wake up at the first sound that wasn't normal. I had developed a sense over the past few years that I had grown to trust. It was like my body would react to any unusual sound or movement. At night I slept with my handgun under my pillow and when I woke up it would be in my hand. I guess it was a developed sense of survival.

As I slept the old dream returned of that first night when the world seemed to come apart. Hours of shaking and rolling with strange sounds and choking dust. There were strange orange glows in all directions on the horizon. I learned from my radio that it was from all the volcanic eruptions that followed the earthquakes.

The only reason my cabin stood up so well was it rested on three cross timbers that extended beyond the end walls. This allowed it to move around quite a lot. Although that first night when the quakes were the worst I thought the cabin and I were both gone. I remember the funny smelling air, like matches smell when first lit. Also, the thick dust that settled down through the air for weeks. At times it was so thick I couldn't see my outhouse, some twenty steps from the door.

Occasionally the quakes still come and once in a while I see a new orange glow off on the horizon but the dust has settled and the sun appears for a short period every day or two. So, with things at least appearing to improve, I lived on.

Chapter 3

The winter passed slow and cold but again with very little snow. I managed to get a few deer and had good luck with the fishing. Keeping those holes open in that thick ice was a real challenge. I never saw another man's tracks or heard any gun shots all winter long.

I passed a lot of time reading and rereading the books I had gathered in my sorties around the area. I had brought a backpack full back from the settlement of Brimson, some ten miles to the east of me. All my life I had loved to read, especially books and novels of the early settling of America.

I had always loved reading about history and it was by far my best subject in school. I know reading so much about the hardships of the early settlers has helped me in my survival now. Especially about men who hunted and trapped to live.

I recall reading a trilogy of books about a mountain man that lived in what would be the Montana and western Dakota area today. It was written by Terry C. Johnston, a great writer of western novels. I believe the time of this mountain man's life that Terry wrote about was between 1820 to 1860. Those were the peak years for trappers due to the popularity of the beaver hat. Up until 1840 you could sell all the beaver pelts you could trap.

After that the beaver fad had died out and the market quickly faded.

The annual big event for these trappers was called a rendezvous. Fur buyers would travel to certain meeting points on the rivers and meet with the trappers to bargain for their furs. Many of the fur buyers were unscrupulous and used cheap whiskey to loosen the trappers' bargaining skills. The buyers usually came away from the rendezvous far ahead in monetary gain.

Johnston went into good detail on how the mountain men lived and survived in the wilderness. Many of these men spent the winters with the Indians and learned their ways. In those times few Indians had rifles so the mountain men's guns provided more game in the winter months. Many took Indian brides.

The mountain men learned of the medicines the Indians made from various plants. They saw Crow women gather spiderwebs from the brush. They were used to put in wounds to aid healing. I recall reading about spiderwebs being used by wounded men in the Civil War, so it must have worked. These were just some of the things I recalled from Johnston's books.

Some of the other writers I had enjoyed reading were Zane Gray and Louis L'Amore. Gray was a great western writer with a romantic flair. Romantic in his sense of description. He could write several pages just describing a distant mountain range, its colors and shadows, and still hold your interest. In his book, Tappan's Burro, he told of a mountain man that loved his little burro so much, he carried it down a mountain in a snow storm. The physical strain caused his death, but Zane Gray made you understand why he did it. Louis L'Amore, in my opinion, was the greatest American writer that ever lived. Many people think of him as a writer of cheap paperback western novels. Granted, he did write a lot of those, but late in his life he produced his finest work. The series of the Sackett family was outstanding. He touched on Indian spiritual beliefs in *The Haunted Mesa* and *The Lonesome Gods*. Some of his writings had nothing to do with the West. *Walking Drum* was a great book about camel spice trains crossing the Arabian deserts. *Last Of The Breed* was about a downed American pilot that escaped Russia by crossing Siberia in the winter.

He was truly a diversified and extremely talented writer not just of novels but also of poetry. I had a copy of *Smoke From This Altar*, a book of L'Amore's poems that I treasured. I recall in the last pages of that book he said, "I think of myself in the oral tradition – as a troubadour, a village taleteller, the man in the shadows of the campfire. That's the way I'd like to be remembered – as a storyteller. A good storyteller." I think he was one of the best.

I also enjoyed reading books of the Civil War era. Two of the best that come to mind are, *The Killer Angels* and *The Bloody Ground*. I didn't think any tragedy would befall this country worse then that war but I was proven wrong some three years back. I think some of the worst military decisions in world history were made during the Civil War. General Lee's decision to have Pickett charge at Gettysburg and McClellan's failure to follow his own officers' advice and charge a vastly outnumbered Lee at Sharpsburg and end the war rank as worse military decisions than the Charge of The Light Brigade. Such bad decisions allowed a terrible war and dreadful loss of life to go on far longer then it should have.

Now that I look back I can't recall man learning anything from war other then to work to prevent it. I guess it does make for great books and points for military people to argue over for time to come.

Chapter 4

The winter passed slow and hard, although maybe a bit warmer then the past three since things went to hell. The need in me to talk to someone, to see another human seemed to grow with each passing day. I felt if I had survived maybe others had. I decided when I was sure the weather was starting to warm I would do some searching.

It looked like spring was finally arriving in what I thought to be very late May or possibly early June. I decided to try heading south first. That was where more people lived, so it made sense that's where the best chance of sighting other survivors would be. I would try to make it to an area called Island Lake. I think it was actually a man made reservoir. It was quite large with lots of cabins and a few year-round homes along the shores. I recall it had several islands and was split by a paved county road bridge. There was a bar and restaurant where the county road hit the north shore. It was called the Island Lake Inn. During the deer hunting season my friends and I used to stop there for burgers and a beer. I remember they used to put on a contest hunters could pay to enter for the biggest deer shot during that season. We always took some chances but never did win it, although we did enter a two-hundred pound ten pointer one year. It was a friendly place that did a good business during the deer seasons.

So, after a few days preparation, I rose early one morning and got ready to head south. I had my backpack ready to go. I decided to take both my .270 and the .22 handgun. I filled the clips of both and had twenty rounds for the rifle and fifty for the automatic in the backpack. Also in the pack was enough smoked fish and venison jerky to last a week. I figured I could make Island Lake in two days easy.

I first headed west for a couple of miles to hit what was left of a paved road that ran south to Island Lake. After I got headed south the going was much slower then I had anticipated. The road was split in many places with cracks and sometimes deep and wide crevices. I was forever sidetracking into the woods to get around deep holes in the road. The skies were overcast as always so I had to rely on my compass on numerous occasions to get back to the road. I knew it was about twelve miles to Island Lake but I began to realize I would have to walk twice that far to get there.

Just before dark I saw a good spot to spend the night just off the road. From my memory of driving the road many times in past years I figured I'd only traveled about four miles. I felt like I had walked twenty. I was too tired to start a fire so I dug out some smoked fish, rolled out my sleeping bag and lay down to relax. I lay on my sleeping bag in the gathering darkness thinking about finding other people, hoping they would be nice folks, hoping they would accept me. As I dozed off I recalled something from my high school days that Eliot had written, "The end of our exploring is to arrive where we started and recognize the place for the first time." Damn strange the things a man remembers.

The next day was uneventful except for my getting wet in a spring rain. That night after covering maybe five miles I built a good fire and dried my clothes and boots. I dug out the old journal and got caught up. Shortly after I had crawled into my sleeping bag there was a series of sharp tremors but I had become so used to the ground moving so often I just went off to sleep.

Toward dusk the next day I knew from the country around me I was within a couple miles of Island Lake. I started to pass scattered abandoned houses so I started looking through them for anything I could use. From the looks of it they had been gone through several times in the past. After following an overgrown driveway well back into the woods to a small house I got lucky. I found a closed gallon can about half full of sugar and in the back corner of a storage closet I found eleven rounds for my 30-30 that I had left back at the cabin. I felt sure I'd be going back there so I took the shells. It was nearly dark so I checked one more house where I figured to spend the night. It was there that I found a true treasure, five rolls of toilet paper. I found myself chuckling while I thought how something so simple could become such a welcome sight to a man. I settled in for the night knowing that tomorrow morning I would reach Island Lake. I sure hoped I'd find someone.

The next morning after wrapping all my new found treasures and hiding them in a dry culvert under the road, I started out for Island Lake. I figured if I didn't locate anyone I would be coming back this way so I could pick up my things then.

I didn't get but about a quarter mile when the sound of a rifle shot froze me in my tracks. I judged it to be a large caliber, maybe a 30-06. It had that distinctive sound big guns make, a kind of ka-boom rather then just a boom sound when they go off.

It had come from the southeast, maybe a good mile off. I stood and waited a few minutes in case there was another shot but it didn't come. I started out again and in less then an hour I saw the lake. I was relieved to see it was just as I remembered it. I had visions of finding it empty or something due to the quakes but it had survived in good shape. I decided to work my way west along the shore toward the bar and restaurant about a mile or so away. As I moved along I checked the cabins for anything I could use. It was apparent they had been searched many times. Most of the doors had been kicked in and lots of the windows were broken out. I found little I could use.

I got to the Island Lake Inn and was disappointed. It had burned and collapsed in a charred heap of rubble. The search of the houses and cabins around the Inn proved fruitless.

I sat on a rock on the shore to think the situation over when I noticed the bridge connecting the road that crossed the lake was completely gone. That took care of any plan to keep walking south unless I took a boat. It was then I realized there were no boats. I was pretty sure the Island Lake Inn rented fishing boats but there were none. As I looked along the shore there were no boats around any of the cabins either. This struck me as being very strange. I knew some cabin owners take their boats home but many just tip them over on the shore or in their yards. None were to be found.

Having found no one and nothing of value to me I decided to head back the way I had come. I'd gone about a mile when I smelled it. It was faint but definitely wood smoke. The smell of burning wood carries a long ways when there is a breeze.

The wind was from the south so I walked down near the shore of the lake trying to pin down the source of the smell. I could see no smoke anywhere along the shore. My mind told me there must be a connection between this morning's gunshot and now the wood smoke.

A wary feeling started to set in as I headed east along the shore trying to pin down where the smell was coming from. I stayed back in the pines staying off the open shoreline hoping I would see them before they saw me. I knew now I was real close to other people.

As I was moving along I looked out at an island near the center of the lake. I saw something silver in the brush along the shore. I sighted the spot through my rifle scope and it definitely was two fishing boats pulled up into the brush on the island.

I sat down to ponder the situation. Whoever was on that island probably was the one that fired that shot this morning. Also, I figured out why there were no other boats around. For security on their island they must have sunk all the other boats on the lake. They had created their own private fortress.

After watching the island for some time and seeing no movement or any more smoke, I decided to continue along the shore to the east. With any luck I hoped to find where they had been landing their boat. If I could wait and catch them ashore I could approach them from a safe distance.

I tried to stay out of sight from the island. If they had gone through the trouble of sinking all those boats they must have had problems with strangers in the past.

I found their landing site about a quarter mile down the shore. There was blood and deer hair, people's tracks and signs of many boat landings. I read the tracks to be two men and a large child or woman. From the look of it they landed their boats here all the time. It was a good spot that couldn't be seen from the nearby road.

Darkness was about an hour away so I headed back into the pines to spend the night. I had some venison left for supper that I would make due. I didn't want to fire a shot even if I saw game or make a fire that could be seen from the island.

Just at dark I returned to the shore and put my rifle scope on the island. They had a small fire going and I saw two figures moving about through the trees near the fire. I was excited at the sight of other people and wanted to yell out, but that instinct I had developed these past few years took over and I calmed down. Just seeing other people would have to be enough for today. I headed back into the pines to my sleeping bag feeling better then I had for a long time.

The next morning brought no change. The island was quiet, and both boats remained where I first saw them. I could only wait them out, knowing they eventually would run out of meat and would come to shore to hunt.

I had noticed a few more shore cabins and what looked like a year-round home further down the shore. I decided to check them out while waiting for action from the island. I found nothing in the cabins but signs of vandalism from previous searchers.

The year-round home proved more interesting. It was obvious there had been a gun battle here. The living room window faced the driveway coming in from the county road. The front of the house was riddled with bullet holes and all the window glass was shot out. On the inside, the floor near the front living room window was littered with shell casings from a .243 rifle. In the back bedroom, the windows were also shot out and 12 gauge shotgun shells littered the floor. It was apparent the home owner had tried to hold off one or more of the roving gangs that had pillaged the countryside after the quakes had subsided. From all the blood on the floors, a good fight had been lost.

The next place I checked was cleaned out like all the others but didn't show any signs of violence. It also had a small barn and a garage well toward the rear of the property. There were a few tools in the barn, but it was in the garage that I hit it lucky. Up in the rafters was a small canoe. It had two small holes, but a little pine sap and some pieces of birch bark would make her water tight in no time.

My mind flashed to the island and those people. I now had my way to get out there. However, food had become my number one problem. I was down to next to nothing and had to hunt. That meant using a gun and not wanting the island people to know of my presence, it meant getting out of hearing distance. So I headed northeast, trying to put distance and thick woods between me and the island while watching for game.

About three hours later I was passing around a swampy area with cat tails and a few open water channels. I heard a slight splashing sound and froze in a crouch. Two pairs of mallards came into view maybe fifteen yards away. They hadn't seen me and were passing left to right. I knew a rifle shot might still be heard back on the island, but felt they would never pick up the sound of my .22 automatic. The lead duck was a big drake. I steadied the handgun with two hands across my knees and fired. I hit him just behind the breasts. His companions took off and disappeared to the south. The water was close to three feet deep and I hated getting wet with a cold night ahead. I retrieved and cleaned my duck, then started a nice fire. I slow cooked that duck on a green branch while I dried my clothes. It was a fine fat bird and I was set for a couple of days.

That night as I lay in my sleeping bag I tried to think what would be the best plan to approach the Island. How to get there without catching a bullet, or hopefully without even being seen required some thought.

Chapter 5

My final decision was to go to the island late at night. I figured if I arrived after midnight chances are no one would be awake. If they found me in the morning sitting there in front of them they would figure I meant no harm.

I would go with just my handgun and hide that somewhere near where I beached the canoe. That way I would appear to them to be unarmed and peaceful. If things turned bad maybe I would be able to get back to the canoe and the gun and have a chance to defend myself.

I packed up my gear and the remaining half of the duck and headed back to repair the canoe. By late afternoon I had the canoe repaired and carried down close to the shore of Island Lake.

I passed the rest of the day hidden but periodically checking the island through my rifle scope. I only saw one man briefly through the trees and near dark there was smoke above the trees. I couldn't determine much about the man other then he was about average height and build.

Due to no time piece I had to guess when midnight arrived. While waiting I hid my rifle and sleeping bag and checked the clip in my automatic. I also took a compass bearing on the island. The night was real dark but the four direction points of my compass glowed just enough to be read. I sure didn't want to paddle by the island in the dark. Thinking it was time, I shoved off. I couldn't see the island but I knew it was just a couple of points west of straight south.

The wind was light and from the southwest, so I hoped it would carry what little sound I made away from the island. I was feeling like I was starting out on a great adventure, yet the thought of these people sinking all the other boats brought on an apprehensive feeling. I guess the years of loneliness built up within me overcame my fears and I paddled on.

After I had checked my compass the fifth time the island suddenly loomed up in front of me. The shore in front of me was full of large rocks that I had not seen from shore. Apparently I had ended up on the west shore instead of the north. As I got real close I could see thick norway pines rising out of thick brush just behind the shore line rocks.

I quit paddling and watched and listened. I didn't see or hear any signs of life. Then I quietly turned to the right thinking that was the direction of the two boats I had seen from shore. After a while it became obvious I was wrong. Frustrated, I started looking for a place to land. Quietly I put ashore on a little gravel strip between two boulders. Then I lifted the canoe and carried it up onto dry land. I was in the trees and apparently had made it without being seen or heard. I stood still and listened to the night sounds for a long time. All was as it should be.

The thought of leaving my gun here by the canoe weighed heavy on my mind. The decision to keep it or leave it could mean my life. Finally, deciding I would be much better received if unarmed, I hid it in a crack in the rocks. Then slowly I started moving forward through the trees toward the center of the island.

Going through the woods at night is a slow and perilous thing.

I moved very slowly, trying not to make the slightest sound. My idea was to enter their camp, then sit and wait for them to find me in the morning. I hoped them finding me without a weapon would prove I meant no harm to them. As I moved I eased each foot down feeling for any twigs or branches. If I felt something I would shift my weight to the other foot and try again.

In about twenty minutes I came to the edge of their camp. It was a cleared area about fifty feet across. On the far side of the clearing I could see a shed like structure that had a tarp roof. Next to the shed was a large tent, maybe ten feet across the front. Over to my right I could make out the front of a smaller tent. In the center of the clearing was a stone surrounded fire pit with metal grates over it. There was still a small fire burning in the fire pit and it cast some light on the front of the three structures. The doors of the three were closed with tarps and there were no sounds from any of them. I edged my way to the side of the fire and sat on the ground with my back against a pile of split wood. I could now hear the muffled sleep sounds of two people coming from the large tent.

My feet had gotten wet when I had lifted the canoe out of the water so I put them up close to the fire to dry. I was exhausted with the heat from the fire warming my feet I must have dozed off.

A loud voice startled me awake. "Wake up, fella." My eyes shot open to find the man who had spoken standing across the fire pit. He was tall and thin but appeared very strong. He wore a deer skin jacket and had a short beard like mine. His hair was cut short and he had no hat. I guessed him to be in his early forties. In his right hand was a large pistol pointed toward the ground.

We looked at each other for a couple of minutes. Then another man, older then the first, emerged from the smaller tent wearing only his pants. "What the hell, where did he come from?"

he said. About that time, a woman's voice inquired of someone named Cal, what was going on out there?

I figured I had better start talking so I said, "I got in last night and didn't want to wake you good folks." The man across the fire said to the older man, "Jeb, I guess if he wanted to do us in he could have done it during the night. You check and see if he's got a gun, then we'll hear his story." The man named Jeb took the rifle the woman was now holding through the flap in the tent and told me to stand up and put my hands behind my head. I did as I was told and he checked me good. "He hasn't got a gun or a knife, Calvin," he said. "Now you sit back down and tell us just what you're doing here."

I told them my complete story. How I had survived the quakes and eruptions. Learning what had happened from my radio. Fishing and hunting to stay alive, and even the reason for coming to their island. My need to see other people. When I had finished they were silent for awhile, thinking about me.

The woman broke the silence. "Everyone we have had anything to do with for a long time has brought us nothing but pain and grief. The last man we took in cost me the life of my daughter. He raped her, then killed her to keep her quiet. My husband Calvin found him covering her body with brush. He tried to shoot him but took a bullet in the leg. So he got away."

The man called Calvin then told in better detail how it had happened and how due to the lack of snow, they had been unable to track the man. Jeb said he had searched for a week but not a sign of the man could be found. Then Calvin from across the fire said something that startled me. "I'll always know his track when I see it," he said, "No man but him leaves a bar across the middle of his right boot print."

"I've seen him," I said. They showed an immediate reaction. "Where?" Calvin asked.

I told them about seeing the man that past fall. How he had acted with extreme caution. Calvin said he figured the man thought they were still after him. Jeb asked if I was going to return to that area. I told them I had planned on it but due to not seeing the man again for the whole winter, I figured him to be long gone.

Chapter 6

The fact that I had told them of seeing the man they hated so bad put me in good stead with them. Jeb built up the fire and the woman produced some great biscuits with some kind of jam made from a mixture of berries. God, it was unbelievable. They couldn't help but notice the expression on my face when I took that first bite of biscuit. Even the woman smiled at me. Then much to my delight she put an old coffee pot on the grate over the fire. My first smell of coffee in a long time.

They asked me what I liked to be called. I told them my name was Dirk Volcots. The woman said to call her Jenny. I could still sense a feeling of apprehension whenever she spoke to me. Also I couldn't help but notice she watched my every movement.

It turned out Jeb and Calvin were cousins and both owned cabins on the lake. In the winter they stayed in Jeb's cabin which was more secluded and offered the best security of the two. In the summer they gave up the comfort of the cabin for the security of their island. Jeb said they stayed on the island until the lake started to freeze. The ice fishing was pretty good in the winter and they did well catching walleyes. I told them of my little lake and the sunfish and crappies I caught. I couldn't help but notice they didn't give any actual location of Jeb's cabin.

I guessed Jeb to be ten years or more senior to Jenny's husband Calvin. Maybe late fifties to sixty, but in good shape. Just hearing him talk for a few minutes revealed his obvious higher education. Cal, although the younger of the two, was the leader. I think the more intelligent Jeb let that happen because he knew Cal was the more outdoor type.

As that first day passed my first impression of the two men held true. Jeb had headed the Geophysics department at a university, retiring the summer before the eruptions and quakes had started. He had taught courses in all fields of Geophysics for many years. His head full of knowledge of meteorology, volcanology, and was actually an expert in the field of seismology. I had a million questions for this man.

Calvin was as I had read him. He had been working for the Minnesota Dept. of Natural Resources. He was an expert on fish and game. I immediately made plans to pick his mind on things that would help my survival.

Jenny, I found to be loaded with know-how when it came to edible plants and preserving things. She had come from Chippewa ancestry and had been very active in the Indian Community for most of her life, trying to preserve Indian heritage for future generations. Her knowledge of the old Indian ways had proven invaluable in their sudden return to a primitive way of life.

They told me they only left their island when they needed food or fresh water. They shot game for meat, gathered wild berries, harvested wild rice in the fall, collected maple syrup in the spring and fished year around. From their great physical appearance I judged they had been doing quite well.

Calvin told how Jenny could make a stew out of roots and venison that was delicious, and asked me how long it had been since I had a helping of cranberry sauce.

Jeb laughingly said, "I've learned never to ask what's in it, but it's usually quite tasty."

I wished I had paper and pencil to take notes on what I was learning from these people. I was trying to remember every detail because it was going to make my survival so much easier.

Late that day the three of them talked it over and invited me to stay awhile. I returned to shore and retrieved my rifle and other gear. That night Jeb produced a rubber mat to roll my sleeping bag out on. He even invited me to sleep in his tent but I told him I preferred to sleep by the fire.

As I lay by the fire that night after they had gone to bed I felt relaxed and figured I had been accepted by this little group. Accepted by Calvin and Jeb anyway. In the case of Jenny, I knew it was going to take some time to gain her trust. They all seemed to get along quite well. The only time I had seen any of them get uptight was when the Bar-Track man came up in the conversation. At the mention of him, Calvin's face took on a cold look of hate. I guess I could understand why, seeing as the man had raped and murdered his daughter.

The next day and those that followed were filled with learning. I found out what was in the stews and soups that were so tasty and nourishing. Jenny told me how she had taught the men to harvest the wild rice that grew in the surrounding lakes and marshes. She showed me the shallow pit that they lined and then thrashed the rice by stomping and grinding it around with their feet. Then they would throw it in the air and let the wind blow away the chaff. Rice was the mainstay of their diet.

It seemed I had arrived just before the maple syrup season was over. The next day we all went ashore in the two boats. It was about a two mile walk to the area of maple trees they had tapped. Jeb showed me how they tapped the trees by driving in a grooved hardwood spike that he called a spile. Although they used pails and kettles they had found in the abandoned cabins to catch the syrup, Jenny showed me how the Indians made containers by folding birch bark. She told me you could boil liquids in birch bark containers, as long as enough liquid stayed in the container it would not burn through.

We transported the syrup back to the island in buckets. There the syrup was boiled down and stored in glass containers. It seemed like three-quarters of the syrup was lost in the boiling process. As a treat Jenny continued to boil a small amount until it started to crystallize into a maple sugar candy.

Jenny loved to talk about the Indians from the past. She told of how the women and children gathered plants, berries, roots, and the maple syrup. The men and older boys were relied on to supply the meat. It was really hard for an Indian armed with a bow and a knife to bring down a deer. Jenny explained how the woods or eastern Indian carried a short bow with a maximum range of about forty yards. They actually had to get as close as sixty feet to get a sure killing penetration with their arrows. In comparison, English long bows could cast an arrow over two hundred yards. Indian bows were well cared for and were rubbed down with melted fat and animal oils to keep the wood sealed. They were always unstrung and carried in an animal skin case when not in use.

The woods Indians were skilled in trapping and building snares to capture small animals. They knew the fish came into shallow water to swim up the streams to spawn when the ice was melting off the lakes. Jenny told me how she seasoned and smoked her fish and other game.

I made the comment about what a wonderful way of life the Indians had in northern Minnesota. Jenny replied, "Yes it was, until 1854. That's when the Treaty with the Lake Superior Chippewa was signed." She went on to tell how the white man wanted the tall pines and the minerals so he took them. Since no Chippewa spoke English, translators employed by the government were used. The Chippewa didn't know what they were signing away.

The Boundary Waters Chippewa, the Bois Forte Band, were allowed to live on four tiny reservations: Grand Portage, Fond Du Lac, Nett Lake and Lake Vermilion.

To make sure the Indians could never return, the 1964 Wilderness Act included the definition that wildernesses were places where humans did not live but merely passed through on a transient basis. This, in spite of the fact that the area had been the homeland to numerous Indian bands for over 8,000 years. Jenny's head was full of Minnesota Indian history.

Another thing the group collected for eating was cranberries. Jenny had a way of preserving them and they were delicious.

I recalled being told years ago that a cranberry bog existed somewhere near the little lake I now fished in the winter near my cabin. I thought, when I get home I'll go find that cranberry bog. That thought shocked me. I had called my little cabin home when I always referred to it as my hunting shack in the past. Thinking of it made me miss it. I hoped everything was all right back there.

A few nights later as we sat by the fire, I told the group of my thoughts of home. Jenny said, "No matter how humble it is, home is always home, a place of comfort to return to."

Her statement put us all in a sad and lonely mood. All of our thoughts were of homes we would never see again, family members we would never see again.

All was quiet around the fire when Jeb spoke, "You know God knew all this was going to happen. I won't say he made it happen, although he may have." I asked him what he meant and he replied, "All this destruction, all the people dying except a chosen few to begin again." When asked why he thought of that, he said, "It was in the Bible." He then started one of the most stirring quotes from memory I've ever heard:

"And the dead shall be thrown out like dung, and there will be no one to offer comfort. For the earth will be left empty and its cities will be torn down. None will be left to till the ground and sow it. The trees will bear fruit but who will gather it? The grapes will ripen but who will tread them? There will be vast desolation everywhere. For one man will long to see another, or to hear his voice. For ten will be left, out of a city, and two out of a field, who have hidden in the thick woods or in holes in the rocks."

With tears running down my face, I asked, "Jeb, where did that come from?"

"The Second Book of Esdros," he replied. "Perhaps we are the blessed few that were picked to survive."

"Blessed or damned, I'm not sure," Calvin said, as he rose to head for his bed. Jenny, with tears in her eyes, kissed Jeb on the cheek and followed Cal to bed. I laid back on my sleeping bag and dozed off, looking at Jeb's sad face in the flickering firelight.

Chapter 7

Many nights I passed sitting at the fire absorbing some of the many facts Jeb had in his head regarding earthquakes and volcanic activity. He was convinced the two were related. He had a fantastic memory for facts and figures and was a fascinating man to listen to. He said proof that earthquakes and volcanoes were related was a matter of historic record.

He told me that in 1857 an earthquake measuring eight on the Richter scale of magnitude, struck the Los Angeles area of southern California. At that same time Tres Virgines in Baja, Mexico erupted. Mt. St. Helens and Mt. Lessen also erupted about that same time. Then about a year later Mt. Ranier and Mt. Baker showed volcanic activity. So you have the coincidence of a major earthquake in California happening about the same time as volcanic eruptions in Baja and along the Cascade Range.

More proof the two are related came in 1870. That year the biggest quake in several hundred years struck Owens Valley. At the time of this quake there were major eruptions of the Sierra de san Andreas and Mt. Colima volcanoes in Mexico. Also about this time, Mt. Ranier and Mt. Baker again showed volcanic activity.

In the nineteen hundreds quakes and eruptions coincided in

1915 and 1940. There were quakes in these years in the Imperial Valley, the Mojave Desert, the Mammoth Lakes area and in Mexico along the northern part of the Golf of Mexico. At the same time, volcanoes were active at Colima in Mexico and from 1914 to 1917 Mt. Lassen erupted. Also in 1941, Mt. St. Helens and Colima showed activity.

Jeb also pointed out that the frequency of earthquakes has been steadily increasing. This was also a matter of public record that had gone ignored although just looking at the figures would tell anyone of a coming disaster. From 1880 until the 1940's there averaged only 2.3 earthquakes per decade worldwide above a Richter 6.0 reading. In the 1950's there were 9, in the 1960's there were 13, in the 1970's there were 51, and in the 1980's they jumped to 86. Then in the 1990's they increased to over 100 in the first five years and tens of thousands were killed around the world.

I said, "Jeb, I don't recall ever reading in the papers anything about such an increase in quakes."

He replied, "Well, you were a typical member of the public then, because every quake of any significance was reported in the papers. I know because in the classes I taught the students were required to check the daily papers for reports of quakes or volcanic activity anywhere in the world. Then we would discuss them and any time spans between quakes and volcanic eruptions, if any occurred."

Jeb said, "Yes, the public simply ignored the warnings of the steady increase in quakes. After all, this is the same public that ignored the fact that using tobacco increases the chance of getting cancer. The same public that put up with failing morality, with rampant crime increases, with dope being sold on the street corners of every American city to destroy the future of our young people. I guess as long as those so called responsible people in government drew their pay checks and lived in those nice homes in the suburbs away from the crime and other problems it would never affect them personally. They took all their materialistic gains as a sign the country must be doing well.

I said, "Yes Jeb, I remember once seeing a bumper sticker on a fancy new pickup truck that read, He who has the most toys when he dies wins the game."

Jeb said, "I wonder if that man sat and looked at those toys as he sat in his big fancy dark and cold house watching his family die from hunger and cholera or some other disease. That is, if his house was still standing."

Jeb was one of the most intelligent and informative men I had ever met. I told him that one night after Calvin and Jenny had retired for the night and left the two of us to our nightly discussion.

He said, "Intelligent only because of my many years of hard study and teaching sometimes brilliant young minds the make-up of this planet we live on. I think any person who is knowledgeable on a given subject likes to share that knowledge with anyone interested in hearing about that subject. After all, what good is knowledge but to share it so someone can learn from it. Wanting to share knowledge has to be in the make-up of any good teacher."

He said, "As far as you complimenting my mind, I would like to compliment you, for being a good quiet listener for these many past nights. I've been doing all the talking and you all the listening. It brings to mind something Mohammed said, "Conversation enriches the understanding, but solitude is the school of genius."

Once again Jeb had managed to impress the hell out of me. It seemed he had someone to quote from for any given situation. I could only imagine how his students must have looked up to him.

Chapter 8

The summer had slipped away and the wild rice season was about to begin. I told the group I would stay and help with the rice harvest. Then I would return to my cabin before the coming winter. I had some firewood left from the previous winter but more needed to be cut. Also, I needed to build up my supply of dried and smoked fish and meat for the days ahead when I wouldn't be able to get out due to severe cold or snow. Jenny told me I would get an equal share of the rice to take home plus some of the syrup and some goodies to help me through the winter.

With that in mind and all that I had learned from these people, I knew this coming winter would be much easier then the past winters. I'll never forget the long cold nights when I wasn't sure where I would find enough to eat.

One night soon after that we noticed a small fire on the shore where we landed the boats. Calvin called Jenny out of the tent. She looked at the fire and said, "Oh, my people are here." Then she gathered a sack of things from the storage building and her and Calvin set out for shore.

Jeb explained to me that the Indians came to visit Jenny every few months since they had taken to living on the island in the summers. They also had visited her at his cabin in the winter. He said, "They think of her as a kind of counselor. Someone to give them advice in troubled times." He added, "They also exchange gifts. You saw the bag Jenny had taken along. Usually they exchange food or some piece of clothing."

I inquired if I could go over and listen in but he said, "No, you better stay here. Cal even stays near the boat, out of hearing range of the meetings." Jenny had told them her Indian friends were there to seek her guidance and we were not to be a part of it.

It was about three hours later that Jenny and Cal returned. Jenny said, "My people told me the rice crop is going to be better this year. They think it's due to having a few more sunny days this summer. Also, they say meat is getting hard to find. Their hunters are going further out on each hunt to find game." She then showed us the beautiful deerskin vest they had given her. With that, she went into her tent. I'd wanted to ask her where the Indians lived and how many there were, but she didn't seem to want to talk about the Indians any more so I let it go. She appeared troubled or had a lot on her mind as she left.

That night by the fire a thought occurred to me, why hadn't Jenny enlisted the help of the Indians to track down the Bar-Track Man when they were after him? Surely an Indian could have easily located him. When I asked Jeb why she hadn't, he replied, "She shares her knowledge with the Indians, not her troubles."

The rice harvest lasted nearly two weeks. Jeb and I used the canoe and Jenny and Calvin used a small flat bottom boat that him and Jeb had hidden near one of their rice ponds. It was as the Indians had told Jenny, the rice was better this year then in previous seasons. My share was going to be all I could carry back to my cabin. A half cup of rice boiled in water expanded enough to be an ample meal for a man. If I had rice maybe three times a week, my supply should last most of the winter. It was going to be a great supplement to my fish and venison diet.

To harvest the rice we spread a tarp in the bottom of the canoe. As we moved slowly through the rice we bent the plants over the sides of the canoe. Then we beat the rice off the plants with sticks catching it in the tarp. It didn't take long to get the knack of it. After a couple of days we were outdoing Jenny and Cal.

On two occasions we saw Indians gathering rice in the same area. They never approached us and only acknowledged Jenny's presence with a wave. I couldn't help but wonder if times hadn't slipped back to the whites versus the Indians as in old movies. However, these Indians had never shown any signs of hostilities toward us. I believe our being comrades of Jenny, who they seemed to respect a great deal, had something to do with that.

The task of harvesting the wild rice proved to be more fun then work. We worked the chaff of the rice by stomping on it in lined depressions in the ground. It turned into a dance contest. We all made up our own steps and watching Jeb cracked us all up. The man had some really wild moves. I could visualize him back in his younger days on a college dance floor. He must have really been something.

After we worked the chaff off the rice Jenny used a shallow pan to throw the rice into the air and let the wind blow the chaff away. She was pleased with the harvest and figured the Indians would have a pretty good winter. She always showed concern when Indians came up in our conversations. Jeb had told me she had gone to where the Indians lived on two occasions in the past couple of years. They had summoned her with a fire on the shore and she had left with them, returning after two days both times.

The first time she went was to help an Indian woman having trouble having a baby. The second time she went to help a very sick child. Jeb told me both cases turned out well. The Indian woman had even named her new little daughter, Jenny. Upon hearing this I realized why the Indians respected Jenny the way they did.

Jeb always seemed to know what day of the week it was and the month we were in. The nights had turned noticeably colder and when I asked, Jeb told me it was the fifth of October. I suddenly realized I couldn't remember what year it was. Jeb laughed when I told him and said, "By God Dirk, you've been in the woods too long. It's 2014, almost exactly four years since things went to hell in this old world."

Early the next morning I packed up to head home. Jenny loaded me up with goodies. I had about all I could carry. Then I remembered I had to stop and pick up the things that I had hidden to be picked up on the way back. When I told the three of them about having a stash of toilet paper to pick up on the way home, it got a pretty good laugh.

Jeb said he had something for me and produced two books he said he wanted me to have. One was a collection of short stories by Erskine Caldwell titled the Caldwell Caravan. The other was a James Clavell novel, Tai-Pan. This man and I had become close friends and I choked up. I apologized for not having anything to give him. Jeb said, "Just having you by the fire all those evenings for companionship and what I considered to be a student was gift enough. It was wonderful and I thank you for it."

We said our good-byes and I promised to return in the spring or early summer. Calvin pulled me aside before I left and said, "If you see that Bar-Track man be sure and shoot first. He's a mean bastard and he'll shoot you if you give him any chance." I assured him I would keep my eyes open.

Finally I set out for shore in my canoe. I had told them where I would leave it in case they needed to use it. Part way to shore I looked back at the island and the three of them were standing at the waters edge watching me. They returned my wave and then the sadness hit me. I had found other people and they were good people. People that I could truly call my friends. I knew I would spend many nights in my cabin remembering all those fireside chats I had with Jeb. A lot of the things he had told me about quakes and eruptions I had recorded in my journal and planned to go over them through the winter.

I hid the canoe where I told them I would. It took a few minutes to arrange all the weight I was carrying so it was comfortable on my back and shoulders. I planned on taking a lot more time going back due to all the weight.

The leaves were falling from the trees that were in full fall color. The air was clearer then it had been for a long time. I hoped things had finally settled down for good as far as quakes and tremors went. My whole attitude had been readjusted by meeting good people, learning lots of things about how to survive from them and the lessening of the quakes. Just being able to breathe air without the smell and taste of sulfur was a big relief. I figured the improved wild rice crop to be a sign things were slowly returning to normal.

Chapter 9

I found the place where I had hidden my can of sugar, toilet paper and 30-30 shells. They were all still in good shape. The sugar added another five pounds to my load but I wasn't about to leave it. Jenny had given me some maple sugar but I sure liked the real thing better.

I found with all the weight I was packing I couldn't go very far between breaks. Just getting the pack off my shoulders for a few minutes felt great. My watch battery had given up the ghost a couple of years ago so I guessed at the time. I figured this time of the fall dark fell about seven thirty or shortly after and dawn was around six in the morning. At least I could guess and be within an hour or so, and if I did catch a glimpse of the sun I could figure it pretty close. I had an old alarm clock at the cabin that I kept wound up when I was there. It ticked kind of loud but it gave a kind of homey feeling to the place, especially at night.

On my third break for the day I figured it to be time for lunch. I pulled some jerky out of the pack and some little cakes that Jenny had given me. They were made with wild raspberries and some kind of nuts. They were sure good. I was really bushed from all that weight so I let myself take a little nap.

In an hour I was on my way. The trees were beautiful in their fall colors but the terrain was getting real tough to travel in. I recalled this area from when I crossed it this past spring. There was little straight road left and again I had to spend a lot of time working my way around numerous crevices.

The weight had taken its toll so I figured I'd only covered about five miles. I started to look for a place to spend the night. I found a pine covered little knoll that overlooked a small stream that would do just fine. I dropped my gear under the pines and walked down to the stream stripping to the waist. The water was ice cold but it felt great to get washed up. I noticed the stream fell into a ravine about twenty yards to my left. It made a pleasant sound as it tumbled down over the rocks.

I was exhausted, so after a light supper I was ready for bed. I knew my senses weren't as keen as they were before spending the summer on the island so I rolled my sleeping bag out well back under the pines. In minutes I was asleep.

I was instantly awake with my automatic in my hand. There had been a sharp crack, but not from a branch. It had been a small caliber gun and very close. It seemed like I had just went to sleep but the sun was up. I studied my surroundings for several minutes but didn't see or hear anything.

I was beginning to think my instincts had let me down when I heard it. A faint sound coming from downstream, like someone crying. I crept toward the crevice staying low under the pines. The sound for sure was someone crying. I got to the edge of the crevice and some forty to fifty feet across it sat a boy with his left side to me. He was sitting on a dead-fall with a rifle next to him. He was wiping his eyes with his sleeve but continued to cry.

I went back a ways and crossed the stream to his side. Very quietly I moved up behind him without being heard. I was only a few feet from him when I said, "Hello son."

Startled, he jumped up turning toward me. "Don't hurt me

mister, please." He was scared to death.

I put my handgun in its holster and slowly walked up to him. "I mean you no harm son," I said. "Can I be of some help?" My putting my gun away seemed to have calmed him but from the look on his face I must have been the first man he had seen in a long time. "Why the tears?" I asked.

"I wasn't crying," he said. I smiled at that as he sat back down on the log. "I was hunting and only had two bullets left for my twenty-two. I got one little squirrel but missed the other one and one ain't going to be enough for my mom and me." He continued, "And I know ma is real hungry, even though she sez she's not."

I asked him why they didn't have anything to eat. "He said, "My dad went hunting about three weeks ago and never came back. My mom is real worried because now we don't have anything to eat. I needed that other squirrel real bad. I'd shoot a deer but Dad took the big rifle with him, so all I have is my twenty-two and now all my bullets are gone."

I sat down next to him on the log. He was about thirteen, thin and about average height for his age. He was a nice-looking boy with blue eyes. He didn't have a jacket on and it was pretty cool, so I wondered if he owned one.

He said they lived in a cabin near a small lake about fifteen minutes to the east. They came here to get their water because the stream was spring-fed so they didn't have to boil it before drinking it. I asked if there were any fish in the lake and he replied, "I think so, but we don't have any fishing poles or any hooks." That told me his father was no outdoorsman. Frankly, I was amazed these people were still alive.

He told me they had found the cabin this past spring when they were looking for other people. His dad had decided to stay in the cabin they had found because there were lots of ducks on the lake and he had seen many deer tracks along the shore. The boy said, "My dad's a real good shot and he found this clean stream for us too."

It was obvious the boy was real proud of his father. I told him to come with me and returned to where my gear was. I dug out about five pounds of wild rice and some smoked fish. I had about thirty twenty-two rounds in my pack that I put in his pocket. I had a good supply back at my cabin.

I said, "Son, you take these things and give them to your mom. I want you to tell her I'll be back in three days to help you two out. While I'm gone I want you to gather all the firewood you can. Do you have an axe?" He replied, "Yeah, we got three axes and a couple of saws."

I said, "Good, find all the dry wood you can find and drag it to your cabin. Cut the biggest limbs you can handle off fallen trees and drag them to the cabin. Don't worry about cutting them up for now. When I come back I'll help you cut wood."

He said, "Mister, do you think you could help us find my dad? I just know he's hurt and needs help."

"You take this stuff to your mom. I'll look for your dad on the way to my cabin, and when I get back we'll both look." I said that knowing the chance of finding his father alive was very slim.

The thought of my leaving made him scared and he said, "Please don't go. You'll never find us again and when I run out of shells me and ma won't have nothin to eat." He now had tears in his eyes and a desperate look on his face.

Putting my arm around his shoulders I sat with him on a log. I asked him what his name was and he replied, "David is my name, but everyone calls me Davey. My mom's name is Mary, Mary Finn. My mom said we're Irish."

I said, "Well now, Davey Finn, you've done a fine job of providing for your mom and yourself while your dad's been away. Now you go to your mom and you tell her a man named Dirk will be by in a few days to lend a hand." I added, "And don't you worry about me not finding you. I had picked up that trail to your cabin before I found you."

With that I pulled on my backpack, gave the boy a reassuring squeeze on the shoulders and headed for my cabin. I could hear him running through the woods behind me to tell his mom the good news about finding someone to help them. As I passed the spot where I had first found him I noticed he had forgotten his squirrel. I left it figuring he would be back for it.

As I walked along, I thought about the boy's father. If he had been gone three weeks chances were he probably had an accident. I had my doubts if he was still alive. The boy telling me they didn't fish because they didn't have any fishing gear proved his dad was no true woodsman or survivalist. Making something to catch a fish was pretty basic. Also, the fact they had run out of food so soon after he had disappeared showed me they were not prepared for the coming winter at all. Had I not stumbled onto the boy, they surely would have been in for a prolonged, cold death in the coming weeks. I hoped that boy did as I told him and gathered all the wood he could before I got back there. Oh well, I'd find out in a few days.

After about an hours travel I came to a crossroads where a road sign still stood. When I saw it I knew I would have to spend another night in the woods before I reached home. The sign read "Three Lakes Road" and I knew it was nine miles to my cabin from here. That's nine miles if the road was good but now I knew it would be more then twice that. I really didn't mind because the weather was good and I had met another person. I was looking forward to lending the boy and his mom a hand.

The next morning was crisp and clear. The October air was cleaner then it had been in a long time. I'd gotten started at the crack of dawn. I knew I was now within a day's travel from my cabin. I was happy to see deer track in the area. Some were small so I figured them for yearlings so at least in this area they appeared to be multiplying.

About mid-afternoon I reached the gravel road I headed east on to my cabin when I saw a track I didn't like. A large wolf had walked through a soft area just off the road. It appeared he also figured on dining on some venison in the coming winter. The track was frozen in the muddy ground so I couldn't tell how fresh it was. I was certain it couldn't be more then a week because the nights had just started to get cold enough to freeze the surface of the ground. I hoped he was alone, because if he was part of a pack they would decimate the local deer population in a few weeks. I figured if I saw his tracks again maybe I would set out some bait and get a shot at him.

My cabin was a grand sight. It was exactly as I had left it and it appeared no one had been near it. I had left a small piece of paper in the top crack of the door that would have moved if anyone had opened it and it was still in place. A few mice had moved in so I ushered them out the door with a broom. My bedding I had hung from the ceiling so the mice couldn't get to it but it smelled musty from being closed up in the warm cabin all summer. I took it all outside and spread it out on tree limbs to air out in the cool breeze. I then hung my wild rice and smoked meat from the same ceiling hooks. I didn't want the mice to ruin my winter supply of goodies I'd packed all the way back from the island. I then put my four jars of maple syrup on the shelf, thinking what a treat one of them would be for the boy and his mom.

It was nearly dark by the time I was settled in. The bedding smelled lots better after being out in the fresh air for a few hours. I started a fire, lit some candles and even got the old alarm clock going again. I was back into my old routine and it sure felt good.

I got out my journal and caught up on my meeting the boy and my promise to return to help them out. With that thought I remembered the boy not wearing a jacket, so I looked through several coats I'd found in cabins over the past few years that I thought I might need someday. I found a good heavy one that was a little small on me that would do the boy just fine. I also came up with some good warm gloves for him.

Chapter 10

I was up at the crack of dawn and took a survey of my winter firewood supply. I was in pretty good shape with about a six week supply left from last year. I figured about a weeks work would put me in good shape so I spent most of the day cutting wood. About an hour before dark I headed down to the lake for a needed bath. The lake was getting pretty cold but sure was invigorating. I fished until dark with some new baits Cal and Jeb had given me. I tried some small jigs for crappies that Jeb had called flu-flus. The color yellow did the trick and I headed for my cabin with four nice crappies for my supper. I planned on coming back and getting some to smoke for the boy and his mom tomorrow. After a great supper of fried fish and a little boiled wild rice I sat on the step of my cabin enjoying the cool night air and the quiet of the woods. Mentally I thought I was in better shape then I'd been since the eruptions and quakes. I had things to look forward to. I would go and help the boy and his mother get through the winter. Then in the spring I would return to the island. I planned on asking Jenny, Cal and Jeb if I could bring the boy and his mom to live with them. I knew they would agree to it but wanted to ask first.

The next morning I was fishing just after dawn. They were still biting pretty good and by ten I had a nice bunch of crappies. I returned to my cabin and fired up my smoker. The boy and his mom were going to have some fresh smoked fish. I would have to show the boy how to make a smoker for meat and fish and maybe even show them how to make jerky from deer meat and pemmican from their jerky.

I had read somewhere that the mountain men gave the name jerky to the strips of dried meat they got from the Indians. To eat it they had to bite down hard on it, then jerk it to break it off.

Minnesota Indians didn't know what salt was until the white man came, so they didn't soak the meat strips in a brine solution before hanging them to dry. The Indians just hung the strips of meat over a low fire or hung it on poles out in the sun. Hanging in the sun required about two weeks to get it dry enough to be stored. Drying over a fire took about twenty-four hours.

Modern jerky is made with all kinds of things to flavor it, such as soy sauce, liquid smoke, onion powder, garlic and God knows what else.

I went through my fishing stuff and picked out some things the boy could use for fishing the lake he said their cabin was near. I also checked my ammo supply I had accumulated from checking abandoned homes and cabins. I had an abundance of .22 bullets so I put about fifty rounds into the pack I was making up for the trip back to see the boy.

The thought came to me to give the boy my 30-30. His .22 was too light for anything but squirrels and rabbits and they definitely needed some venison to get through the long winter. I hated to give up the 30-30 because it was my only backup; if my .270 went down I would be without a rifle. Also, that gun had been a gift many years ago from my grandfather, actually he was my step-grandfather. He was one of the nicest people I had ever met. I was closer to him then my own father so that rifle meant an awful lot to me.

I decided I would let the boy use the rifle on a loan basis with the understanding I would take it back when I needed it or if I came up with another gun for him. I recalled Calvin on the island had about six or seven rifles in their storage shed and I thought maybe I could get a rifle for the boy from him. I know I had seen a couple of 30-30 rifles among those he had. So I packed two boxes of 30-30 ammo into the backpack. I had quite a few knives so I put one of those in also.

Two mornings later I set out for the boy's cabin. It was a fine cool morning and my spirits were up. I had everything I could spare in my backpack for the boy and his mom. I had maple syrup, wild rice, jerky, smoked fish, clothes for the boy and ammo. I had to smile because here I was under another heavy backpack and I promised myself on the way back from the island I'd never do it again, yet here I was again.

I arrived at the place I had met the boy near the little waterfall late that afternoon. I followed the well traveled trail for about fifteen minutes and just after detecting wood smoke in the air, sighted the cabin through the pines. It was an A-frame type cabin about seventy feet back from the water of a small lake. It was a pretty setting and I couldn't help but notice the big pile of tree limbs and deadfalls the boy had dragged into the clearing near the cabin.

I called out, "Hey Davey, it's me Dirk." The door of the cabin burst open and out came Davey at a full run.

He shouted, "Hi Dirk," and looking back over his shoulder at the woman now standing in the doorway of the cabin, said, "See Mom, I told you he would come back." He carried the pack I had taken off and we walked to the woman in the doorway. Davey said, "This is my mom Dirk."

"Hello Mrs. Finn," I said, "It's a pleasure to meet you." I

reached out my hand and after a hesitation she offered hers. She spoke very softly.

"I thank you for coming. I've been worried about how we were going to live since my husband Tim has been gone so long. Davey has done his best but with winter nearly here I've been sick with worry. He said you would help us find Tim. I hope you will because I'm sure he's out there somewhere waiting for help to come."

I said, "I sure will do my best Mary, now let me show you what I brought to help you folks out." I started unloading my backpack. Mary hugged the two jars of maple syrup to her breast. She said, "Where on earth did you get this?"

I said, "It's a long story that I'll tell you later."

She then marveled at the big bag of wild rice I handed her and couldn't believe it when I produced real white sugar. I had brought her about half of the can of sugar I had found in that cabin on my trip to the island. I then told her I had just caught and smoked some fish for them and gave her the packet.

Davey asked where I had caught them. I told him about my little lake and then dug out the things I had brought for him.

The jacket and gloves were big for him but the socks and boots fit just fine. His eyes opened wide when I handed him the bone handled hunting knife and sheath. All he owned was a small jackknife so he hung that new knife right on his belt.

I got to the fishing gear and showed him the hooks and jigs. I told him we would try the fishing on his lake tomorrow. His face was beaming. It reminded me of the look on a child's face on Christmas morning.

"Now Davey," I said, "I want to talk to you about something else I'm going to loan you to use. You can't survive here in the wilderness without a rifle big enough to bring down a deer. I am going to loan you my spare rifle. It was a gift to me from a man who was very special to me. A man I was very close to and will never forget, my grandfather. I have a plan to get you a rifle in the spring, but until then I'll loan you this one." I handed him the 30-30 with the side mounted scope.

"Gee Dirk, I promise I'll take real good care of it for you. My dad's got some oil and stuff here so I can keep it clean and real nice for you. You'll have to show me how to load it and stuff. Can we shoot it tomorrow?"

"Sure Davey," I replied, "We will do some shooting and some fishing tomorrow, but we are also going to make that wood pile grow. You're going to need more then you have there to make it through the cold that's coming."

Then Mary said, "I'm sorry, Dirk, in all the excitement I didn't think. You must be hungry. All I can offer is some rabbit we have left from supper, but you're welcome to it."

I said, "Sure Mary, but let's all set down and I'll tell you about the nice folks I spent the summer with."

We sat down at the table and I ate rabbit while they tried some of my smoked fish. From the way the fish disappeared, I didn't think they had time to taste it. I told them all about my time spent on the island. Davey was full of questions about the Indians. Mary wanted to know about Jenny. What she looked like, how old she was, and how she knew all about cooking things found in the wilderness. All the while we talked Davey kept looking at that rifle. I knew I had sealed a friendship.

When we had sat down to eat I noticed a place setting at the head of the table where neither Davey or his mom sat. When Mary went out to the outhouse I asked Davey about the place setting.

He said, "It's for when my dad gets home. My mom leaves it there. It's just one of the funny things she does now. She hardly talks anymore and just sits looking at the fire at night. When she goes to bed I hear her crying but I don't know what to say to her. When Dad was here she talked and laughed all the time. They used to swim in the lake almost every night and we all had fun. Now she just sits or cries. Dirk, I don't know how to help her."

"Davey," I said, "It's hard when someone that's close to you goes away. Maybe now that I'm here we can work at cheering her up."

Davey said, "Yeah, now that you're here and we don't have to worry about food and stuff maybe mom will feel better. Dirk, I told her you were going to help find dad too."

About then Mary came back in and said, "Time for bed, Davey. You go out and wash up. I think you should thank Dirk for all the wonderful things he brought us."

"Yeah, thanks Dirk," Davey said, "This is just great. I can't wait until morning to try out all my new stuff." He then brought in some wood for the fire and went back out and washed up. His mom gave him a peck on the cheek and he said good night as he headed for his bed in the loft.

There was a bedroom in the rear of the cabin where Mary slept. She brought out some blankets and said, "Dirk, if you like you can sleep here on the rug by the fire. You must be exhausted from carrying all that stuff here for us. I want you to know how much I appreciate it. I feel better then I have for a long time now that you're here. How long to you think you're going to stay?"

I replied, "I'll stay until we get you enough firewood gathered for the winter. I'll take the boy hunting and from the sign of deer in the area, we should be able to get you a good supply of venison. I'll fix you a drying rack to make jerky on and show you how to make some other things too. I'm only a full day's walk away so I'll try and come back every couple of weeks and check on you two."

She asked, "Will you try and find my Tim? Davey said you

were going to."

I told her every time I was in the woods hunting I would watch for any sign of him. I told her that was the best I could do because I had no tracks to follow and had no idea what direction he had even gone the day he disappeared. I told her that, knowing full well there was little chance her Tim was still alive. Yet, I didn't want her to give up hope and become more depressed then she already was.

She thanked me and went off to bed. I watched her as she walked away. She probably had always been a small woman but now she appeared weak and frail. I guessed she hadn't been eating right, probably since her husband had left. Also, I was sure the worry about surviving with a young boy to look after had taken its toll.

I lay back on the blankets and let my mind rerun the day's events. I was glad I had returned to help Davey and his mom. It seemed good that I had a kind of responsibility toward them now. It kind of gave my life a new purpose. I was looking forward to teaching Davey to hunt and fish. I guess I wanted to know for myself if there were some nice fish in this little lake. Well, tomorrow I would find out. In minutes my weary body gave way to sleep.

Chapter 11

Davey and I were up and out at dawn. The boy was all fired up. I told him the first thing we would try was a little fishing. We walked the shoreline of the little lake to each of the four other cabins that were on the lake. We found two overturned small aluminum fishing boats and found that one of them had a good set of oars stuck in under the seats. We threw in two poles I had cut from a tree and rigged with line I had brought from my cabin. I rowed and had Davey watch over the side for the weed line. We found the weed line started in about nine feet of water. I explained to Davey that pan fish usually stayed in or near the weed line. Also when predators, such as northern pike look for a meal they hunt the weed beds.

We worked along the shallow side of the weeds using different colored crappie jigs. In the first hour we caught several sunfish that were too little to keep. We located the deep side of the weeds in about fourteen feet of water and tried our luck there. In about ten minutes Davey hooked about a pound crappie on a yellow flu-flu jig. That boy's smile was a mile wide. I kept the boat in the area and we quit with nine nice fish in about an hour. I had found a usable wire live net in one of the cabins so we left our catch hanging off the end of the boat when we hit shore. Davey ran to get his mom. He was now a great fisherman and wanted his mom to know.

Mary was just as excited as the boy and offered to clean our catch and fix us a nice supper. We accepted her offer because Davey was real anxious to fire his new rifle.

I found a small metal bucket, walked off fifty yards, and hung it from a low branch of a bush along the shore. I showed Davey how to lever and load the rifle. I demonstrated how to put the hammer on half-cock safety and shoulder the gun. I had him shoot using a tree branch for a rest. He shot right of the bucket. He tried again and it went right again. This time I noticed he was pulling the gun right when he squeezed the trigger. I took the gun and put a hole in the bucket, not to show off, but to show the boy it was him and not the sights. His fifth shot hit the bucket and then he got consistent. We quit after about twelve rounds. I told him, "Tomorrow we'll try to shoot at something that's moving."

"Great," Davey said and ran with the bucket to show his mom his marksmanship. I hoped she hadn't counted the number of shots and compared it to the number of holes in the bucket. But I did have to admit the boy had done pretty well.

That night we had a great fish supper. As we were eating I told Mary how her son was learning to be a good woodsman. She surprised me with a strange look and the comment, "When my Tim gets back I'm sure he will appreciate what you have taught the boy."

Again, the place had been set for Tim at the table. After the table had been cleared Mary withdrew into her shell and sat by the fire with her arms around her looking into the fire.

Before dark I walked the shoreline of the little lake looking for deer tracks. Across from the cabin I found a long wooded ravine that ran from the shoreline to the east for a good half mile. There were deer tracks of several different sizes that came from the ravine to the lake. Apparently the deer were using the ravine for cover to come to water. Up on the right side there were several large boulders about sixty yards from the shoreline. I figured I would fix that up for a brushed in stand for Davey. With a little trimming he would have a clear field of fire to where the deer came out of the ravine.

Before bed Davey and I walked down to the lake to wash up. I told him about the area that I had found, and what we were going to do. I explained to him that it was best to try and shoot bucks instead of does. That it would mean better hunting in future years if the does were left to have fawns.

Davey asked, "Dirk, if we shoot all the bucks, how can the does have fawns?"

I explained to him, "One buck can make twenty does have fawns. But keep in mind you'll have to shoot a doe if you need meat, and right now we could use the meat. All I'm saying, Davey, is take the bucks first." He understood and we headed for bed.

That night I heard Mary crying for a long time. In the morning she was still sleeping when Davey and I left to go fix up our deer stand. We took along some rope, an axe and a small saw. In a couple of hours we had a pretty good set up. All the brush had been cleared from the line of fire and I had even fixed a log between the boulders for Davey to rest his rifle on to steady it for a better shot. I left Davey to watch for deer while I went to get us something to eat. We had made a lot of noise, so I doubted if he would see any deer for a few hours or even the rest of the day.

When I got to the cabin, Mary said we were out of clean water so I grabbed a bucket and headed for the stream. I was nearly there when a sudden movement caught my eye. A small spike buck moved across the trail about a hundred yards ahead. I put down the bucket and slipped the .270 sling off my shoulder. The well-traveled path I was on allowed me to move without making any noise. Also the wind was blowing across the trail between me and the deer so he couldn't pick up my scent. I moved forward a few steps at a time. After about ten minutes I spotted him in some low brush and scattered pines off to my left. He was browsing with his hind quarters toward me. I crouched and put the scope on him. After what seemed like an eternity he finally turned sideways to his left. I put the cross-hairs behind his left front shoulder and fired. He leaped into the air and collapsed in a heap. I chambered another round and watched where he had gone down. After giving him several minutes I walked up to him. He was a fine young buck taken with a perfect shot.

I wished Davey was with me but I was sure he had heard the shot. He could have learned how to dress the animal out and helped me with the drag back to the cabin. Although I hadn't come that far it took nearly an hour to reach the cabin.

I thought I would go and get Davey to help me hang the deer. I was tired from dragging the deer so I didn't feel up to walking around the lake to get Davey so I pushed the boat off the beach and rowed over. When I got to the far shore, Davey was waiting for me.

Davey said, "Dirk, did you hear that shot? I think it came from behind our cabin. Maybe it was my dad."

I said, "No Davey, that was me, and I got us a fine deer."

I thought he would be happy about the deer, but he appeared almost let down. I guessed he was hoping it was his dad who had fired the shot.

He helped me hang the deer in a tree next to the cabin. Knowing his mom and him now had lots of meat to eat put him in better spirits. I showed him and his mom how to peel the hide off and cut out the tenderloins before they dried. We then pulled the loins out of the back before quartering the animal and hanging them out of reach of any animals in a shaded area. The weather was cool enough now that spoiling wouldn't be a problem. There was more ice on the lake shore every morning now.

The next couple of days I spent building a drying rack for meat strips over the wood stove and building a meat smoker out of a little barrel I found in one of the cabins around the lake. I showed Mary how to scrape the hide and rub the deer's brain tissue into it. She seemed happier if I kept her busy. I think it kept her from thinking about her husband Tim.

Davey still managed to get the boat through the shore ice every day to get out to fish. He was developing a talent for it and we had the smoker going nearly every day. Between fishing trips Davey would take the boat to the far shore and sit in his deer stand.

The weather was getting colder but the snow had held off. It must have been a week after I had shot my deer and about mid-morning when I heard Davey fire his rifle. He had left for his deer stand just after dawn. I listened for a few minutes but he didn't shoot again. Hopefully, he had dropped one with a single shot.

He had taken the boat so I set off on foot around the lake. When I got to his stand he was gone but there was a shell casing on the ground. I listened for awhile and finally heard him up the ravine. In a few minutes I saw him standing with his rifle up looking through the scope. He didn't shoot so I walked up to him and asked him what happened.

He said, "Two deer came down the ravine in front of my stand. The second one had big horns and I shot him. He fell down and I thought I had him but then he jumped up and ran this way."

I said, "Davey, lets go back to where he went down and see if we can pick up a blood trail. If you hit him hard enough to put him down I'm sure he's hurt pretty bad." We found where the deer had gone down with no trouble. There was hair and dark blood on the grass.

I pointed it out to Davey and explained to him he should always wait a few minutes before pursuing a deer that has been shot. I said, "A wounded deer will almost always lay down in the first good cover it can find. Then if it's hit good it will bleed out and die."

We picked up the blood trail and I had Davey walk off to one side but told him to keep me in sight and never move ahead of me. Davey was really pumped up and in a few minutes I motioned to him to come and see a place where the wounded deer had laid down and left a pool of very fresh blood. I quietly told Davey we were getting close and to be ready. We again moved ahead and in a few minutes I spotted his horns moving above the edge of a deadfall. I motioned to Davey and he spotted him as he got to his feet. Davey fired and the deer went down for keeps. We slowly walked up to the animal and found the boy had shot a nice eight point buck.

I instructed the boy on the proper way to dress out the deer and let him do it by himself. Davey went back to his stand and got some rope. Together we dragged the deer to the boat and loaded him up. All the way across the lake the boy kept retelling me how he had first shot the deer and how his mom was going to really be happy now that they had all the meat they could ever need. We had to break through about thirty feet of shore ice in front of the cabin to beach the boat. I knew our days of using the boat were about over.

Davey hollered for his mom to come. He was one proud boy when he told her not only had he shot the deer, but had gutted it out all by himself.

We hung the deer in a shaded cool spot near the cabin. It was nearly dark so I figured on cutting him up in the morning. I did cut out my favorite, the tenderloins for a great supper.

That night as I sat by the fire I began to think about heading home. These folks now had a pretty full larder and with Davey adding a few fish every few days or maybe a rabbit or squirrel they should be in good shape for quite awhile.

By the next evening we had the drying rack over the stove loaded with strips of venison. It took a good twenty four to thirty hours to dry the meat enough to be stored. After it was dried we tied it in bundles and hung them from the rafters for future use.

The quarters of venison we hung in the shade of the pines well out of reach of any varmints. The weather was cold enough now that the venison stayed frozen. I showed Davey how to saw off portions for his mom when she needed it. They had enough venison hanging from the two deer we had killed to last a long time.

That night when we sat down to supper I told them I planned to head home the next morning.

Davey said, "Dirk, you can't go. We need you here with us. Besides, you haven't looked for my dad like you promised."

I said, "Davey, I will be back in a couple of weeks. You and your mom have plenty to eat and plenty of firewood until then. You can work on the hides like I showed you. Maybe your mom can make a jacket or coat for herself with them."

I explained to them that I wanted to get back to my cabin because I had lots of supplies there that I had gathered through the years from the cabins and homes I had visited. Also, I still had a good supply of food there including a lot of wild rice I had carried back from the island.

At this point Mary said, "Now Davey, if Dirk feels he wants to go, we must let him. Lord knows we now have plenty to eat, thanks to him. If he says he will be back in a couple of weeks, he will. Remember he said he would come back when you first met him and he did."

Davey said, "Yeah, I guess so, but what about trying to find Dad?"

"Davey," I said, "Every time I'm in the woods, and that will be every day the weather lets me, I'll watch for any sign of your dad." That seemed to satisfy the boy.

Davey got up and said he had to visit the outhouse. I went out for some air and stopped him on the way back to the cabin. I said, "Let's sit and talk for a minute, Davey. I have some things to say that I don't want your mom to hear because I don't want to upset her."

He said, "Alright," and we sat down on a log.

"Davey, your dad has been gone too long just to have been lost. I know it's hard to think it but I think you're better off to begin facing that fact. I will do as I promised and keep looking for him but if I do find him, I don't think he will be coming home."

"Oh God," Davey said, with his eyes filling with tears.

I put my arm around him and said, "You're the man of the family now, Davey. You've learned to shoot game and catch fish. You and your mom are well supplied for now, but you can keep adding to it. You are going to do just fine without me and I promise to be back in a couple of weeks."

Davey said, "I guess you're right, but I hate to see you go."

I said, "You're going to be just fine, but there is one thing I want you to do while I'm gone. Whenever you leave the cabin, always carry your rifle. If a stranger shows up, question him from a distance. If you want, give him a little food if he asks for some. Just don't let him get close to you and don't let him into the cabin. What I'm saying is, be careful of strangers. Davey, you don't have much, but in these times there are those who have less and will take all you have."

Davey said, "Okay, but I don't think anyone will come around in the winter. Say Dirk, before you go, do you think you could draw me a map so I could find your cabin? Just in case my mom gets sick or something and I have to find you."

"I sure will," I said, "And I'll even mark the trees with an axe so you can follow it real easy."

With that, he seemed to feel better so we washed up for bed. I told him, "Now don't mention what I said about your dad to your mom. She isn't real well as it is and hearing something that might upset her sure won't do her any good. I do think time and not having to worry about food anymore will help her to get well."

Davey said, "I sure hope you're right. I know she's worried about me not getting any schooling too."

When we got to the cabin I said to Mary, "In the spring I'm going to take you and Davey to the people on the island that I told you about. Jeb, one of the men there, is a fine teacher and I know he would enjoy teaching Davey. He told me he misses teaching a lot. He used to teach in a big college and he's a real expert on earthquakes and volcanoes. I think Davey and him would get along just great."

Mary said, "That's sure what the boy needs. My Tim tried his best but we didn't have any books or anything to help teach him. He can read fairly well but that's about it."

I said, "Mary, when I come back I'll bring along some books for the boy to read. I've got quite a few I found in the cabins and homes I've been in over the past few years. You could help Davey and by next spring when we get him to a teacher he should be able to read really well."

She said, "Having books would be a great help. I used to love to read and I hope Davey learns to like to read too. Dirk," she said, "About going to the island next spring, I'm not sure I could go until I find out about my Tim. He promised he would be back the morning he left and he has never broken a promise to me."

Not wanting to discuss that now, I said, "Mary, spring is a long time off. We'll see what happens."

She said, "You're right," kissed Davey good night and went off to bed.

Chapter 12

Next morning I got ready to leave early. The sky was overcast and it was colder. I figured we were in for some snow but there was little wind so I didn't look for any big storm.

Before I left I cautioned Davey in front of his mom about going out fishing before the ice was safe to walk on. I told him to cut and carry a long pole with him if he did go out. That would help him out if he fell in. I told him I would probably be back by the time the ice was safe to walk on but I knew how young boys think.

I set out for my cabin still early in the day. Mary, who didn't think my axe marking the trail would be good enough for Davey to follow, had provided me with a spool of red ribbon to mark the trail with.

I figured I was over half way when the snow and the wind started to increase. The wind was from the northwest and felt like it was getting colder by the minute. I picked up the pace figuring the first good winter storm was closing in. I was traveling lots lighter then when I was headed the other way carrying food, clothes for Davey and the two rifles.

Finally I hit the gravel road that ran east to my cabin. I knew I was only about a mile and a half away from shelter and a nice warm fire. The snow was coming down heavy now and there was at least three to four inches built up on the ground. I figured my traveling a lot lighter had cut over an hour off the trip home.

I quit marking the trail when I hit the gravel road. I had told Davey I would double mark the last tree where he would come to the road to my cabin. I had told him to follow the road a little over a mile until he spotted the three cedar trees among the birch on his right. There he should turn right and walk in about a hundred yards to my cabin.

The reason I didn't want to mark the trail closer then a mile from my cabin was that you never knew who might follow the trail.

I reached my cabin about twenty minutes later. I couldn't tell with all the fresh snow if anyone had been around. I checked my little door trick and no one had opened it since I had left. All appeared well and it felt great to be home.

After getting a nice fire going, I hung my damp clothes over the stove to dry. I had brought back about ten pounds of venison loin and I sliced off three pieces and put them in a pan to cook. I got down my wild rice supply and put a good half cup in a pan with some water. I was famished from the long walk.

After supper I filled a big pan with snow and melted it on my wood stove. After it had melted and warmed I took a good sponge bath and put on some fresh clothes. When I tossed out my bath water the snow was still coming down heavy. The wind had really picked up and I couldn't see but maybe a hundred feet. It was great to be clean, warm and comfortable in out of the weather.

I sat down and brought my journal up to date in the candlelight. While writing about how I taught Davey to hunt and fish I realized how fond of the boy I had become. He was basically a pretty intelligent kid and seemed to pick up on things pretty fast. I figured his father must have been a pretty good man.

I felt I didn't have to worry about Davey and his mom with the snowstorm. They had ample firewood and food for at least a month. The one thing about this storm was it almost guaranteed they wouldn't have any surprise visitors.

Having caught up my journal, I blew out my candles and crawled into my bunk. The wind was moaning as it drove the heavy snow through the pines. In minutes I fell into a deep and dreamless sleep.

Morning found the snow had let up to light flurries. The wind had gone to the southeast and I knew that meant the low pressure area had moved off to the east taking the heavy snow with it. Now I figured I was in for a few days of real cold that almost always followed a good snow storm.

All my life I had maintained an interest in weather and its relationship with nature and especially wildlife. I was always fascinated to watch wildlife adapt to the changing of the seasons. I think my growing up in Minnesota and being an outdoors type person enabled me to watch this in its greatest extremes.

Here you could enjoy a warm summer evening out on the lake in a boat fishing. A few months later you could be fishing in the same spot but this time you would be in a fish house that was sitting on two feet of ice and surrounded by deep snow.

My watching wildlife and how it prepared for the changing seasons became like a hobby. The word they use for the study of wildlife's relation to weather and the changing seasons is phenology. I always worked outdoors and in the fall I would watch for the wooly bear caterpillars to appear. They were easily found on roads and sidewalks in the early fall anywhere in Minnesota. They were brown and black and the thickness of the center stripe was supposed to be an indicator of the severity of the coming winter. The size of the fall acorns was also considered a way to predict how bad the coming winter would be.

One of my favorites was if the muskrats built their houses in deep or shallow water. Deep water was supposed to mean the coming winter would be unusually cold. The theory was that in a severe winter thick ice would block the underwater tunnel the muskrats used to get into their houses. So if they thought a real cold winter was coming with thicker ice they would construct their houses in deeper water.

I guess it was just a fun thing to do and lots of folks in Minnesota seemed to pay attention to it. I always thought in general the people of Minnesota were more knowledgeable about weather then any other state. Again, I think it's due to radical changes that always seemed to take place. One day in the winter it could be forty above and the next morning twenty five below zero.

There is an old saying I truly believe applies to Minnesota – if you don't like the weather, wait a few minutes, it will change. But since the quakes and eruptions things had radically changed. That first summer after the worst of it, the leaves on almost all the trees froze before they were hardly open. The food chain for insects and animals had to have been altered. The leaf eaters had no leaves to eat. Insects and birds that ate the leaf eaters had much less to eat. This no doubt accounted for the fact there were far fewer birds in the forest then years ago. Also, even field mice were very scarce. I do believe this past summer, which was somewhere near normal, did help wildlife to begin a comeback. I sincerely hoped so, because nature's food chain included me.

I had forgotten to start my wind-up clock when I had gotten home yesterday so I wound it and set it for eight o'clock. It was a guess, but it had been light out for about an hour so it had to be pretty close. I just opened the door to go get some wood for the fire when I heard it, the long howl of a wolf. It came from the southeast. I listened and in a couple of minutes it howled again. I was pretty sure from the direction that it was the same wolf. His call went unanswered and he didn't howl again. I figured it was the same wolf that had left the tracks I had seen on the road.

Late in the day the wind quit and the skies cleared. It would probably turn real cold for awhile. It usually did after a heavy snow. I figured it had snowed between eight and ten inches.

I had hoped the ice on the lakes would have a chance to thicken enough to be safe to walk on before we got a heavy snow. Now the ice had eight inches of insulating snow to slow the thickening process. I was glad I had cautioned Davey about going out on ice before I left him.

That thought made me realize I was worrying about someone else. It just made things seem better when I had other people to think about. The previous winters had been harder just due to thinking I was alone here in this frozen wilderness. Now I actually had five people I knew might even think about me on these cold winter nights.

I passed the next few days cutting wood and making several trips to the lake. The fishing was pretty good. True to form the weather did turn cold after the snowstorm and I was pleased to find a good six inches of ice on the lake despite the heavy snow cover.

I mixed my meals with fish, wild rice, venison and jerky. The fresh venison I had brought back from Mary and Davey's cabin was about gone so I went hunting. It took three days to nail a small spike buck, although I did pass on a doe that same morning

Out of curiosity about that wolf, I checked the gut pile from the little buck the next morning and sure enough, he had been there. I was happy to see from his tracks he appeared to be a loner. He also had followed the drag trail through the snow to within sight of my cabin. I knew now that he would come to bait if he ever became a problem. I had hung the quarters of that deer well up out of his reach, although I didn't think he would come that close to my cabin.

The weather stayed clear and cold. I made a trip to the lake at least every other day. The fishing stayed at least fair. I had devised a wind break out of three birch poles and a canvas tarp I had retrieved from one of the cabins. The winter sun seemed to heat the dark canvas around me and enabled me to stay out on the ice a lot longer in the cold.

I had accumulated a nice batch of smoked fish but found I was in desperate need of salt. The Indians in the old days just dried their fish without any salt. I sure preferred smoking them after a good salt soaking.

I decided I would venture to the north and check the cabins and houses for salt that might have been missed in past searches. One thing about salt was that it never spoiled.

I headed out in the morning and the weather again was clear and cold. By noon I had checked three places and found two table salt shakers partly full but that was it.

I had come north on what was left of a blacktop road. After making a lunch out of some jerky and a piece of smoked fish I decided to head home at an angle to the southeast through the woods. Hopefully I would spot a snowshoe and have me a rabbit supper. A grouse would be an even better treat but they were damn hard to come by. I hadn't had a grouse in a long time. I think that first year or two after the quakes when all the leaf buds froze on the trees and bushes caused a drastic decline in the grouse population. I had seen very few since.

As I was pushing through a shoulder high thick stand of balsams I nearly fell into a deep depression. I grabbed some branches and pulled myself back. I would have fallen at least twenty feet down a sheer cliff.

The depression was a nearly perfect circle. It was roughly three hundred feet across. The sides were as clean as if cut with a huge knife. For some strange reason the shaking of the earth had caused this nearly perfect circle of earth to collapse.

As I looked down I noticed what looked like a rifle laying across the top of two large rocks. Yes, it definitely was a rifle. I decided to go down and get it.

I dragged several dead trees over and eased them over the edge. They made a make shift ladder so I could climb down into the depression. I made damn sure it was good enough so I wouldn't have a problem getting out.

I climbed down and walked over to the rifle. I saw what looked like a glove and part of a coat sleeve sticking up out of the heavy snow between the boulders. I brushed the snow aside. A man lay frozen under the snow. He had been dead a long time. From what was left of him he had died before the weather had turned cold enough to keep him frozen. I cleaned all the snow away and examined him. The bone below the left knee protruded through what skin there was left.

He must have accidentally fallen into the pit as I had nearly done. He could never have climbed out, as badly hurt as he was. I figured he died of pain and thirst just before the first snow came.

I checked the rifle. It was an old .243 and it was empty. He must have fired all the shots he had hoping someone would hear them and come to his aid.

I went through his pockets and found nothing. Then his belt buckle caught my eye. It had three letters stamped into it, T-I-M. I then realized I had found Davey's father. Now I knew why Tim had never made it home. The poor soul had died a lingering, painful death. There was little that I could do with what remained of the frozen body. I took his belt and the rifle. I dreaded the thought of having to tell his wife and son how he had died. At least now Mary could maybe get her head straight with the knowing that Tim was gone and she didn't have to sit and worry about him anymore.

I thought I should say something before I left him. I had never met him but felt close to him, I guess from knowing his wife and son. I wished Jeb had been with me, he always knew the right thing to say for any occasion.

I knelt down, put my hand on him and said, "Lord, I've never met this man, but I know those he died trying to provide for. They are kind and gentle people who loved him dearly. So, Lord, I believe this was a good man. Take him to you. Amen."

I climbed out of that hole and wiping the tears off my cold face, headed for home. As I walked my thoughts were of Mary and Davey. I decided I would gather together some supplies and if the weather looked good in the morning, head for their cabin. Somehow I felt they were now my responsibility.

I reached my cabin a little before dark. After I had my supper I started putting things together for the trip in the morning. At the last minute I remembered about the books I had promised Mary I would bring for Davey.

I knew from talking with Mary that Davey could read but not really well. With that in mind I went through the piles of books I had collected from the homes and cabins through the years. Also I wanted something that would hold a boy's attention. I had a couple of C. S. Forester's books from his Hornblower series and selected one titled *Mr. Midshipman Hornblower.* I also picked a book of selected Jack London short stories that any young man would surely enjoy.

After catching up on my diary in the candlelight I went to work cleaning up the .243 rifle I had taken from Tim. I got most of the outside rust cleaned off although there would be some minor permanent damage. The action and the rifling in the barrel showed no damage at all. I attributed that to the rifle having been well cared for and properly lubricated.

I hoped Davey's dad had some ammo for the .243 at their cabin. I knew Davey was going to treasure having his dad's rifle to remember him by.

Chapter 13

Morning came with a light southwest wind and overcast skies. It was damp and warmer then the past several days. In Minnesota, warm days in winter usually meant that snow wasn't far off. I only hoped it would hold off until evening and not be anything major.

I had two pair of snowshoes I had found in cabins but in this heavy brush country I found them to be a hindrance rather then a help. If the roads were still intact they would be great but with only small stretches of roads left I was better off without them.

I headed for Davey and Mary's cabin early. Again I had a pretty full pack and the rifle for Davey in a deerskin sheath tied to it. As always, I carried my .270 and had my .22 auto in its holster.

The trip was pretty uneventful except that the snow had started to fall when I was about half way. By the time I had their cabin in sight there was at least three inches of soft wet snow.

I was still in the woods when something brought me to a stop. The door of their cabin was wide open and no smoke came from the chimney. I got a real bad feeling in my stomach.

My instincts took over. My heart wanted me to run across the opening to the cabin but the instinct I had developed held me back. I slowly searched the surrounding area but saw nothing out of the normal. I heard nothing but the usual sounds of the woods. I dropped the pack in the snow and took the .270 off my shoulder removing the deerskin cover. I edged towards the cabin watching for any movement through the windows. There were no tracks coming from the cabin in the freshly fallen snow.

I reached the cabin and peered inside. Slushy snow had been tracked into the cabin and the tracks had frozen from the fire going out and door being left open.

As I looked at the tracks the hair on the back of my neck stood up. There had been two men here. One had left very large tracks and was wearing boots worn nearly smooth. The other track was from the Bar-Track man. No doubt about it. A perfect round bar impression across the instep of the track. Well, it now appeared he had a companion and quite a large one, judging from the size of the track.

I now figured they were long gone. From the looks of the cabin they had carried off anything they could use. It had been completely ransacked.

I wondered what the hell had happened to Mary and Davey. I hollered out the door thinking or I guess you could say hoping that they were hiding in the woods. All was quiet. My bad feeling was getting worse. I got the fire going, and checked Mary's bedroom in the back. There was nothing there.

I went up to the loft where Davey slept and there I found Mary. Her naked frozen body lay on Davey's bed. Her hands were tied to the headboard. She had been beaten severely and obviously raped. Her head was pressed against the headboard and turned sharply. Her neck must have been broken. There were no bullet or knife wounds visible, so the broken neck must have killed her, but only after she had been put through hell.

I covered her and for some reason found myself saying aloud,

"I'm so sorry, I'm so sorry."

I felt I was to blame. If I only would have stayed maybe I could have prevented this. I even recalled thoughts I had before I left them of taking them with me. Davey wanted to see my cabin but for some reason I had decided they would be all right here.

The thought of Davey sent me downstairs and out the door hollering his name in all directions. There was nothing but silence. I refused to believe he had left his mother to the mercy of those two men.

I was on my knees in the snow. My hope was Davey had gone to find me and somehow I missed him on the trail. Then I reasoned this had to have happened at least three days ago. He would have surely found my cabin because of the marked trail.

I retrieved my backpack and returned to the cabin. It was nearly dark and there was nothing I could do until tomorrow. I got some blankets off Mary's bed and laid down on the floor by the fire. I felt responsible and terribly lonely. My mind was filled with hate for the two that had done this. I vowed to make them pay with their lives. I would find them, if it took the rest of my life, I would find them.

It seemed like I had only slept a few minutes when the morning light was coming through the windows. The fire was nearly out. I put the last two pieces of wood on the coals and walked out to the woodpile. As I was filling my arm with wood I noticed the tips of two boots sticking out of the snow behind the woodpile.

Davey's snow-covered body lay with his head against the woodpile. I picked him up and held him for a long time. I had no coat on so the cold finally brought me to my senses.

I carried him inside and put him on the table. He had taken a bad beating. He had been shot once in the chest. I knew he had done his best but had been no match for two grown men.

I sat by him and pondered what to do with him and his mom. There was no way I could dig a grave in the frozen ground. I even thought of cutting a hole in the ice and sinking them but somehow that didn't seem right.

Finally, a solution came to me. I picked him up and carried him upstairs. I put him down next to his mother and covered them both.

I went downstairs and searched the cabin for anything I would need. The 30-30 with the side-mount scope was nowhere to be found. The two men must have taken it. Also, the wild rice I knew Mary had left was gone. Finding no shells for the .243 rifle I took it upstairs and laid it next to Davey. It seemed fitting, having belonged to his dad.

I spent the rest of the morning hauling all the wood I could find into the cabin. I had it stacked to the ceiling.

I searched for anything that was flammable and stuffed it into the woodpile – paper, curtains, and clothes. Then I lit the pile in several places.

I picked up my rifle and pack and walked out after blocking the door open. I walked out to a dead fall and sat down to watch the fire. In minutes the cabin was enveloped in flames.

I guess I should have prayed for them, but as the fire grew so did the black rage in my heart. My life would have one purpose now. I would use every skill I had developed these past years for one purpose. I must find and punish two men, two of the lowest forms of life left on earth. Two men that didn't know it, but had lost any chance to survive.

As I watched the fire consume the cabin, I remembered something Calvin had said to me when I l left the island, in what now seemed a lifetime ago. He had told me, "When you see the Bar-Track man, shoot first. Don't take any chances. A desperate man is a dangerous man."

Well Cal, I thought, that is not going to happen. I am going to look him in the eye and tell him why I have come to kill him. Tell him why it is right that he must die. That the time has come to pay for the brutal murders of two gentle people, Mary and Davey. Time also to pay for the rape and murder of Jenny and Cal's daughter. Then with the same brutality he used on them, he would forfeit his life.

Chapter 14

I became a man driven by one purpose. I honed my skills as a survivalist to the keenest edge. I worked hard daily at becoming physically tough. I had found snowshoes, next to useless in the brush country that I hunted in, but out on the frozen lake that I fished on they proved to be an excellent physical conditioning tool. I ran the perimeter of the lake nearly every day, regardless of the weather conditions. Within a couple of weeks my stamina seemed nearly limitless.

When the weather looked good I started to take daily ventures out from the cabin in different directions searching for man tracks or any sign of the two men I sought. Spring was just a few weeks away now and I had formed a search plan to use when the weather warmed enough for me to spend one or two nights in the woods without freezing. I would start my search in expanding circles, each time going further and further out, using my cabin as a center point. I still had an old county map that I would use to keep track of the areas I covered.

I felt sure the two men must live in a cabin somewhere within a day or possibly two of where they had attacked Mary and Davey. They no-doubt had just stumbled on their cabin while they were out hunting or searching cabins.

If I looked long and hard enough I was sure I would find them. The thought came to me that if I hadn't found them by the time the ice went out maybe I would take a trip to the island and ask Jenny to check with her Indian friends to see if they had seen the two men. Surely if an Indian had crossed the unusual track the Bar-Track man left he would remember it. But I would not ask their help in actually finding them. That was something I must do myself.

My luck held for the rest of the winter with the hunting and fishing. It seemed that my fishing the little lake seemed to actually be helping the fish population as far as average size went. I recalled the first winter I fished the lake that the pan fish were quite small. Now they averaged about a half a pound apiece on the crappies and the perch and sunfish were also considerably larger too. My thinning them out apparently was helping them to grow.

My wild rice supply was giving out in what I figured to be early March or possibly late February. If I hadn't shared my rice with Davey and Mary it would have lasted until spring.

Just the thought of those two brought back the old pain in my heart. God, how I missed them. My feeling of being responsible for their deaths just never seemed to go away.

My thoughts always wandered to what might have been. How I had planned to take them to the island. Jeb would have had a ball teaching Davey. They would have been great friends.

Chapter 15

Spring came slowly and tested my patience. I wanted to get into my search plan to find the two men. It seemed every time the snow was nearly gone, it would snow heavy again and delay me. This happened four times before an all night warm rain brought winter to a final end.

The ice still covered the lake but all the snow in the open areas was gone. There still was snow in the shaded areas but travel was going to finally be good. I had accumulated a good supply of dried venison and smoked fish. I figured my search patterns would keep me away from home for three to four days at a time. It would be easy to carry food and my guns and still cover the ground I wanted to cover, if I kept to the plan.

My supply of food would last until I had covered the full circle. If I hadn't located the two men by then I planned to head to the island and ask Jenny to make inquiries among the Indians about the two men.

I figured it to be sometime in early April when I left the cabin to start searching. I knew the ice usually went off the lakes in northern Minnesota in late April. I figured my friends wouldn't move out to the island until the weather warmed a little so I thought they would move around mid-May. That gave me five to six weeks to look before heading for the island.

The thought of my three friends on the island brought back a lot of nice memories. I longed to sit again at night with Jeb and have him tell me things about the earth. It was going to be great seeing them all again.

I started my search patterns to the north and gradually moved around to the west, then southwest. After returning from each trip I would mark it on my country map. I was careful to always overlap each search area to eliminate missing any sign of the two men.

Mary and Davey's cabin was to the southwest of me and I was working my way in that direction. I think I was on my seventh trip out when I found myself on the far side of the lake their cabin was on. I could see little of what remained of the cabin I had burned. I knew in a few short years the encroaching brush and pines would hide it forever. I hoped the two people I had left there were at peace. The sight of it renewed my determination to make the bastards pay. I again vowed to never give up until they or I were dead.

With tears in my eyes, I looked back one last time, then headed northeast and home. I had yet to find any sign of the men but I had only covered about one-third of the area I planned to cover.

The ice was out about thirty feet from shore on my lake and I was down to the last three search areas. They were to the east and northeast of my cabin. It was now surely May.

I was about three days out to the east of my cabin when I detected the smell of wood smoke in the air. It was coming in on a breeze from the east and I cautiously followed it.

I came to the edge of the woods near a long narrow lake. There was a row of several cabins off to the left. The smoke was coming from the chimney of the last cabin.

My heart was racing as I carefully worked my way around through the woods to a spot where I could observe the cabin without being seen. There was very little ice left on the lake and the breeze had pushed it up against the shore behind the cabins. It didn't look like it would support a man's weight.

After nearly an hour had gone by, I heard someone leave the cabin by the rear door. I couldn't see him until he came around the right rear of the cabin.

He was huge. He stood nearly seven feet tall, was heavily built, and had a full beard. My mind went back to the big frozen boot tracks in the doorway of Mary and Davey's cabin.

He went into what I took to be an outhouse about fifty feet from the cabin. After a while he came out, looked around, then walked back to the rear door of the cabin. As he walked I put my rifle scope on him but saw no weapon other then a sheathed knife on his right side.

The cabin was about eighty yards from me. The side facing me had a door in the center and the same size windows on both sides of the door. They were oblong horizontal windows, kind of like the old crank outs they put in houses years ago.

It was beginning to get dark so I moved a little farther back into the woods to spend the night and form a plan.

I first had to be sure I had the right two men. Hell, I didn't even know for sure there was a second man in that cabin. One thing that was for sure, I was looking for a big man and I had found one.

I crawled into my sleeping bag but knew I wasn't going to get much sleep. I did a lot of thinking and decided I would watch the cabin tomorrow and see if there was another man. If there was another man that walked with a limp, I would know my search was over. I would give it maybe two days until food would become a problem. There were still patches of heavy wet snow in the shaded areas in the woods so water was no problem.

Dawn found me back within sight of the cabin. I found a new spot where three fallen trees had crisscrossed. I could sit back and look between them yet not be seen from the cabin. I judged it to be about eighty yards to the cabin.

Nothing happened until late morning when the big man came out and walked to a small shed next to the outhouse. He was carrying what looked like a small hatchet. I could hear him chopping at something in the shed and when he emerged a few minutes later, I found out what it was. He was carrying a good sized hunk of meat. They must have a deer hanging in that shed, but from my angle I couldn't see it.

Nothing happened for several hours and my patience began to wear a little thin. Then I heard the rear door close and a much smaller man walked to the outhouse. Walked with a limp.

When he emerged and returned to the cabin, I watched him through my scope. His right boot had metal around the ankle and instep. This was the same man I had seen years ago. The Bar-Track man.

My mind was flooded with thoughts. I had the advantage because they couldn't see me. To leave the cabin they would have to cross open ground. The big man had taken in that meat so they probably had none stored in the cabin. I had access to the venison in the shed and after dark I could go get it. I knew I could outlast them so I figured it was time to force the action.

I cupped my hands and yelled as loud as I could, "Hello the cabin." I put my rifle scope on the front of the cabin and waited.

The big man's face appeared in the window to the right of the door. He was trying to see me but I knew he couldn't. I sat and waited watching the rear corners of the cabin in case one of them tried to run to the woods and flank me. Nothing happened. They were either being careful or were just plain scared.

I hollered again, "You, in the cabin."

This time the door facing me flew open and the big man filled the doorway.

"What the hell you want?" He bellowed.

I put the scope on him. He held a small carbine rifle in his right hand pointed at the ground. I looked at it through the scope and the hairs came up on the back of my neck. The rifle had a side-mounted scope. It was my rifle that this bastard had taken after killing Davey.

With rage building in me, I raised the cross hairs to the center of his chest, and the .270 bucked against my shoulder. He dropped the rifle and grabbed the door frame on each side of him. He slowly sagged to his knees as the Bar-Track man screeched, "What the hell!" behind him.

The big man, chest covered in blood, slumped over backward into the cabin.

All was quiet and I was shaking like a leaf. Dusk was starting to settle in when I noticed the big man's boots move. He was being dragged back into the cabin. I figured the Bar-Track man wanted to move him so he could close the door. Thinking he was to the right of the door and probably crouched down trying to pull the heavy man, I put a round through the wall about three feet off the floor to the right of the door.

"God dam," came from the cabin. I must have come pretty close.

All was quiet and dark closed in. The clear sky held a quarter moon. It was light enough so he couldn't leave the cabin without my seeing him.

I ate sparingly thinking I had better stretch my remaining food. I really didn't know what he had left to eat in the cabin. If worse came to worse and I was still here, I would get me some of that venison from their shed tomorrow night. The moon should be about gone then.

Sometime during the night I dozed off because the noise of a door closing snapped me awake. The door facing me was now closed. He had managed to move the big man enough to clear the door while I dozed. I could see the 30-30 on the steps of the cabin in the moonlight. He must have several guns in the cabin but if I was to need another, there it was.

I managed to stay awake until dawn broke and all stayed quiet. I had made up my mind to let him make the next move. Maybe even make him think I had left the area.

About mid-morning he cranked open one of the front windows. He shouted out, "Why did you kill Big George?"

I didn't answer.

After a few minutes he shouted again, "Hey you out there. What the hell do you want?"

Again I didn't answer him. Over the next few hours he yelled out to me several times, but I remained quiet. I knew it had to be bothering him that I never answered.

It was about half dark when I noticed it appeared to get lighter in the front windows of the cabin. I thought he had probably lit a candle when it came to me. He must have opened the rear door of the cabin and the additional light that came through showed behind the front windows.

He had made a mistake. Had he waited another thirty minutes I would have never known he was leaving the cabin.

I brought the .270 up and watched the rear corners of the cabin. I tried to guess which way he would go.

To the right about fifty feet away was the outhouse and the shed they used to store their venison. All open ground.

To the left was a good sized woodpile, maybe forty feet from the cabin. Behind the woodpile the woods started.

My instinct told me he would try to get to the woods. I was

right. The light was nearly gone when he made a run for the woodpile. He ran pretty good for a man wearing a brace, but never made it.

He was outlined by the light colored shore ice behind him. I fired a single shot and dropped him ten feet from the woodpile. The round knocked him off his feet and the rifle he was carrying flew out of his hands.

He lay with both hands clutched to his right lower rib cage. As I walked up on him I could see dark blood coming through his fingers. From the darkness of the blood I figured he was shot through the liver and I was looking at a man who was soon going to die.

I checked him for weapons then grabbed him by the collar of his coat and dragged him to the woodpile. He was bleeding bad but was conscious. I propped him up against the woodpile and knelt down in front of him.

He looked at me and said, "Why, and who in the hell are you?"

"My name is Dirk," I said. "Why, is because you and that friend of yours killed two people that meant a lot to me. Also, you killed and raped a young girl down at a lake south of here. Her mom and dad are friends of mine. I promised her dad I would look for you. He wants you dead real bad. He made me promise to shoot you on sight."

Looking at me, he said, "You got it all wrong."

I said, "Like hell I do. Her dad caught you in the act. You been running ever since."

He coughed a couple of times and said, "Calvin lied if he said he was her dad. He's her stepfather. I lived with them for most of one summer. Nice folks except for Calvin. I used to catch him watching that girl all the time. She used to swim in a tee-shirt and walk around half-naked. I guess he just finally snapped. I happened on him when he was covering up her body after he had finished with her. He saw me and figured if he shot me he could tell the others I done it. He missed me and I got away only because he fell and hurt his leg. I figured he still told the others I done it so I just kept going."

I said, "I don't believe you."

"Hell, I'm shot clean through. I'm dying mister. Why in hell would I lie?" With that, he coughed some more, bringing bloody froth to his lips.

Suddenly doubt crept into my mind. I thought again of Cal telling me to be sure to shoot him on sight. He didn't want me talking to this man because his secret would be out. Cal had used me. Used me to murder a man.

I said, "What about the woman and the boy? I know it was you and your big friend. That rifle over there on the cabin step belongs to me. You took it off the boy after you bastards killed him."

He was getting real weak and it was getting hard to hear him when he spoke. "That one I guess I owe for. Big George went berserk when he saw that pretty woman. He never was quite all together in the head anyway. I shot the boy because he had the drop on George and was about to kill him with that rifle. George wasn't much but he was the only friend I had. I've never forgotten shooting that kid. I swear, I never touched the woman."

I said, "Why did you let the big guy kill her?"

Between coughing spells he said, "I didn't know he'd killed her till after it was done. Were they kin to you?"

"No," I said. "Just folks I cared about."

A lot of blood came now with the coughing. He tried to reach out his hand, saying, "Sorry, so sorry," and spoke no more.

I sat there thinking for a long time. What he had told me had shaken me. I guess the fact that he knew he was dying and therefore had no reason to lie convinced me he had told me the truth. Also, the fact that he had admitted to his shooting the boy when he could have blamed it on his dead friend proved he indeed was telling the truth.

Calvin had lied. Calvin was living a lie. Now that I thought about it, I had just assumed he was the girl's father. No one had said otherwise.

I owed it to Jenny and Jeb to get the truth out. They were living with a rapist and a killer. They had taken me in and trusted me. I owed it to them.

As I looked over at the Bar-Track man I realized I had never known his name. I walked over and went through his pockets but found nothing other then a compass and a folding knife. Inside of his jacket he had a packet of jerky and about fifteen shells for his rifle.

I dragged him back into the cabin and laid him alongside his friend. I found some candles to light, then searched the cabin for anything I could use. There was very little other than more shells for the Bar-Track man's rifle, a very beat-up 30-06. I couldn't find any other weapons in the cabin. I guess the Bar-Track man must have not trusted his friend to have his own weapon. At least prior to the episode at Mary and Davey's anyway. I did find quite a few rounds for my 30-30.

I didn't feel at all bad about the killing that I had done. The memory of finding the bodies of Mary and Davey prevented any feeling of guilt.

I couldn't get the fact that Calvin had used me to kill a man for him out of my head. If those two hadn't killed Mary and Davey, I would have murdered two innocent men. The thought enraged me. I also figured I had better be careful and try to set up the confrontation so it would be in my favor. There was no doubt in my mind that Cal would just as soon kill me to keep his secret.

I moved what I wanted out by the woodpile and lit a nice fire.

I didn't care to spend the night with two dead men. I helped myself to some slices of venison from the deer hanging in their shed. I hung the strips over the fire and only then realized how tired and hungry I was. It had been a long hard search to see justice served. Mary and Davey were finally avenged. I had fulfilled my final promise to them.

With my belly full of warm venison and a feeling of satisfaction I closed up my sleeping bag and within minutes fell into an exhausted sleep.

Next morning I tied the two rifles to my pack, gathered up the rifle shells, candles and matches that I had found and headed for home. If I really pushed, I would make it before dark. I also had packed what little venison was left in the shed. It wasn't much but would give me a meal or two.

Chapter 16

The trip home went well and I did make it just before dark. I got the fire going and got out a few smoked fish for my supper.

While I ate I cleaned the two rifles I had carried home. I was glad to have the little 30-30 back and to find it still in pretty good shape. I had quite a few shells for it and figured on using it when the shells for my regular rifle started to run low.

The 30-06 I had taken from the Bar-Track man was in pretty bad shape. Even the stock was cracked and had been wrapped in deerskin strips to hold it together. Still, it was a gun, so I oiled it up. Then I wrapped it in a blanket and stuck it up in the rafters. Some day I might have to put it to use.

The candles I had brought back I was real happy to have. I was just about out and having some candles to read by or to work on my diary in the evenings had become kind of a ritual with me.

Finished with the guns, I brought the diary up to date. It seemed strange when I wrote about the two men that I had killed when I didn't even know their names. I put them down as the Bar-Track man and Big George. I knew nothing about them other than the evil they had done.

Again, the thought of Calvin using me came to mind. I figured I would wait at least another ten days before I headed down to the island. By then I was pretty sure they would have moved out there for the summer.

I had warmed up some water on the stove to wash with and had just finished up when I felt the ground move. I walked back to the cabin and was in the doorway when a tremendous roll of the earth put me on my knees. I grabbed onto the door frame and hung on. There was heavy shaking and things were flying all over inside the cabin. I realized I had mistakenly figured the quakes were over and had become very careless about stowing my gear. There hadn't been any quakes for some time.

There were deep grinding moans coming from the earth and the shaking got even worse. It was as bad as I had gone through years back when things had gone to hell. As I clung to the door frame I could see a strange orange glow through the dust filled air off to the northwest.

Then I was suddenly thrown across the cabin floor by a tremendous roll of the earth. The cabin's rear support beam must have slipped off the blocks causing the rear of the cabin to fall. The floor now tilted down about two feet. Luckily, I had the legs of the stove secured to the floor with heavy bolts so it stayed in place.

All around me I could hear trees crashing to the ground. I was glad I had cut down all the large trees around the cabin that posed any threat of falling on it.

It stopped as abruptly as it had started. In a matter of a few seconds all was quiet. I crawled to the door and looked out. The air was so full of dust and debris I couldn't see the birch trees that I knew were fifty feet away. There were heavy booming noises off to the north and northeast. I couldn't see the orange glow anymore, but it could have only come from an explosion or eruption. The air was just too filled with dirt to see anything.

I went out and walked around the cabin. As I had suspected the rear support beam had slipped off the blocks. There was no other damage that I could see. Tomorrow, if I could get out, I would find a piece of timber to use as a lever and get the cabin leveled up again.

There was a heavy smell of sulfur in the air and it was burning the hell out of my eyes. Somewhere up wind of me there must have been an eruption. That was the only thing I could think of to explain the sulfur-like smell.

I got two towels from the cabin and soaked them in water. Returning to the cabin I shut the door and laid down on my bunk. Due to the tilt of the cabin my bunk was at an angle so I lay with my feet on the low end. I covered my face with one of the towels and balled the other one up next to me in case I would need it. The wet towel helped me from breathing in that dirt filled air. It even seemed to filter out some of that sulfur smell.

I fought off a feeling of despair and loneliness. Mother Nature never seemed to quit testing me. I was exhausted and knew there was nothing I could do until daylight. I knew from past experience there probably wouldn't be much daylight for several days.

I slept well past daybreak and would have slept longer if it hadn't been for an aftershock. There were three of them in the space of just a few minutes. Then all was quiet.

I got up and opened the door. There was a fairly strong wind from the west. I hoped it kept up, figuring it would blow all the bad air away.

Enough light was getting through so I could see to work. I kept wetting a towel and wrapped it around my nose and mouth while I was outside. I couldn't do anything to help my eyes and they were soon burning again.

I found a good piece of wood for a lever and worked the cabin floor beam back on the blocks. At least I'd have a level bed to sleep in again. By the time I was done with that my eyes were burning so bad I had to wash them out and get back into the cabin. As long as I kept the door closed the air was a lot better inside the cabin.

I wondered about the wildlife and how hard this must be for them. Surely their eyes were being affected and they couldn't get out of the bad air like me.

I knew the sulfur and falling ash on the surface of the lake wasn't going to do the fish any good either. I hoped the wind kept blowing because it could only help everything. The wind making waves on the lake was sure to carry a lot of the pollutants to shore before it had time to settle in the water.

As I sat there in the candlelight, I found myself thinking about the island and how I missed my friend Jeb. He would surely find this last episode of quakes fascinating. I remembered one night when we were sitting by the fire when Jeb told me all about the eruption of Mount St. Helens. As always, he was doing the talking and I the listening. It was yet another time when he impressed me with facts and figures he had in his head. But then volcanoes and eruptions were his field of expertise.

He told of how the first warning tremors started on the 20th of March in 1980. They increased for a few days into what he called earthquake storms. He explained that to mean, combinations of small and moderate quakes every hour.

On May 18th at about 8:30 a.m. seismometers in the area responded to vibrations coming from a large earthquake under the volcano. Within 15 seconds, shock waves shattered the summit and the north side of the mountain collapsed in an avalanche of rock and ice.

Jeb then told of how seconds later, Mt. St. Helens blew its top. Smoke and ash rose 60,000 feet. The shock wave leveled trees

in a 230 square mile area.

I recalled the intense look on Jeb's face as he looked into the fire as he spoke. He told me temperatures soared to 500 degrees Fahrenheit igniting trees and charring any animal, including the unlucky humans in the area.

The impact of the shock wave sloshed the water out of nearby Spirit Lake. When it ran back in, the lake was 295 feet shallower then it had been just moments before.

I recalled I had asked Jeb how many people had died at Mt. St. Helens. He thought around sixty. He recalled reading about one man that lived and ran a lodge on the shore of Sprit Lake. He had been warned but didn't leave. His body was never found.

I didn't think there had been any real shock wave last night so hopefully nothing the magnitude of St. Helens has occurred. Although that orange glow I had seen surely meant there had been some sort of volcanic activity.

I was thankful the wind continued to blow. The air was starting to get better slow but sure.

As the day wore on the air in the cabin got much better. When I had to go out I made it quick and closed the door behind me. By noon the outside air had cleared enough to see a faint glow in the sky from the sun.

I spent the day straightening up the inside of the cabin that was in shambles. I stowed everything away where it wouldn't go flying if another tremor hit.

As I was putting my books away, I picked up one that I had liked to read whenever I was down and feeling sorry for myself. It was a book of collected poems.

I sat by my burning candles and thumbed through it to the one I had come to believe was written just for me. "Invictus"; I had read it so often I could recite it from memory. It went –

Out of the night that covers me,

Black as the Pit from pole to pole,
I thank whatever gods may be
For my unconquerable soul.

In the fell clutch of circumstance
I have not winced nor cried aloud.
Under the bludgeonings of chance
My head is bloody, but unbowed.

Beyond this place of wrath and tears
Looms but the horror of the shade,
And yet the menace of the years
Finds, and shall find me unafraid.

It matters not how straight the gate,
How charged with punishments the scroll,
I am the master of my fate;
I am the captain of my soul.

With the dawn came the blessing of a heavy relentless rain. It seemed like the power that brought the quakes had a complete change of heart. It had decided to clean up the mess it had created. It washed the dirt off the budding leaves and grasses. It even cleaned the dirt off the cabin windows.

I imagined the birds shaking the dust out of their feathers in the falling rain. The animals shaking their fur free of the clinging dirt. It was like life was beginning again.

The next morning was fresh smelling and bright sunshine seemed to reflect off the leaves that had popped open since the rain.

I had a line of snares and box traps that I had used for years. They all had been set off or ruined by the quakes, so I checked them all and reset the usable ones. I worked my way to the lake wanting to check the shoreline for dead fish. I hoped the falling ash hadn't fouled the water. As far as I could tell the woods animals had survived the ordeal in pretty good shape. Birds were singing and the ground squirrels were playing their usual chase games with each other.

I found it amazing how a good rain could change things around so completely. I got to the lake by mid-day. No dead fish were on the shore or on the water. My fear of the sulfur dust settling on the water and hurting the fish was unfounded.

I did find something very interesting. My wolf friend had apparently gone for a swim. He had left tracks where he had come out of the water. I couldn't see any tracks going into the water so he must have entered somewhere across the lake. I guessed he had wanted to get the foul smelling dirt out of his hair. For some reason I felt it was good he had survived the quakes. I had come to look upon him as a survivor, so we had a lot in common.

I headed back for the cabin checking my reset traps along the way hoping for a rabbit but no such luck. I was almost to the cabin when I did manage to bag a gray squirrel. I liked squirrel better anyway and I think squirrel is better nutrition wise. I guess the only reason I think that is I recall a scene in an old movie about a mountain man by the name of Jeremiah Johnson. In the scene an old mountain man was sharing a piece of a rabbit that Jeremiah had cooked over a fire and told him that a man couldn't live long on a diet of just rabbit. It lacked certain things that other red meat provided. Strange how some things stay in your head.

The weather stayed nice and in just a few days the trees were all leafed out. I decided it was time to head to the island. Part of me said to just let Calvin go, but I knew it would always stay with me that he thought he had gotten away with murder. The murder of someone I thought of as a good friend's daughter. I went about packing for the trip figuring on leaving the next morning.

Chapter 17

The sky was overcast the next morning and looked like rain. As always, I carried my .270, and my .22 auto was in my belt holster. I had cleaned and oiled them both the night before with the thought in my mind that one of them might be needed for my survival in the next few days when I confronted Cal. On my back was a pack with my clothes, some jerky and some cooked meat for my supper. I figured there was no reason I couldn't make the island in two full days so I only carried what I thought I would need. But with my sleeping bag and a couple of books for Jeb, it was a pretty good load.

As luck would have it rain woke me about midnight and I had to find cover under some balsam pines. They didn't provide the best of shelter and I got a good soaking. That plus the fact that it turned cold caused me a delay of several hours in the morning trying to dry out my clothes and sleeping bag over a fire.

The clothes dried but the thick sleeping bag stayed damp. Due to the time spent drying my gear the next evening found me still several miles from the island. I spent the night with the damp sleeping bag wrapped around me by a fire. I paid the price. Morning came and I had a dandy cold and sore throat.

I had only myself to blame. Any good outdoors man knows

that allowing yourself to stay cold and wet for any length of time could result in real serious health problems. Without so much as an aspirin for medication, only warmth, good food and rest would straighten me out.

I sure hoped I would find my friends on the island because that was the only place I was going to find what I needed. Jenny would likely have something to help me. She was an expert on natural medications like roots and herbs that Indians used for any number of illnesses.

I reached Island lake about midmorning. The boat wasn't at the usual spot where they beached it, yet I could see no sign of life on the island. I was in real trouble.

I was shaking with cold so I gathered some wood and got a fire going. I knew I had a fever and had to stay warm and dry. My sleeping bag was still damp so I tied it between two trees behind me at the fire to trap in the heat. I dug through my pack and got out another heavy shirt and put it on. I finally was starting to warm up. Feeling a little better I gathered a big supply of wood in case I had to spend the night here.

I couldn't believe no one was here. The lake and the island looked just as it had when I'd left last fall. The recent series of quakes had not effected them. Maybe something had happened over the winter. I figured I had better start thinking about getting something to eat, and soon.

I figured being here by the lake that fishing would be my best bet. I had put my canoe in a garage about a quarter of a mile away when I had left last fall. I sure wasn't up to carrying it back to the lake today. Hopefully if I kept warm and dry I would feel better in the morning and would get it then.

I settled in by the fire and dozed off. When I woke a couple of hours later there was a misty cold fog coming off the lake. I built up the fire and took down the sleeping bag and wrapped it around me. My throat was so sore it was hard to swallow and my fever was back.

I slept fitfully through the night. I remember being cold and putting more wood on the fire several times. Dawn came with a cold raining mist. My sleeping bag was soaked and I was sweating profusely. Figuring my fever was breaking I put more wood on the fire and tried to sleep.

Someone said, "Dirk, hey Dirk, wake up."

I looked up and Jenny was standing over me. I saw Jeb behind her and heard him say, "Christ, he's nearly dead."

Jenny said, "We have to get him out to the island and into a warm bed as quickly as we can."

My throat was so bad I couldn't talk. I was soaking wet and freezing cold. I noticed my fire was out and looked like it had been for a long time. Jenny told me not to get up and came back in a few minutes with Calvin. He and Jeb helped me up and I found I was too weak to stand alone.

The next thing I knew I was awake and there was a tent roof above me. I knew I must be on the island but I couldn't recall the boat trip. I must have passed out on the way out. I wondered how long I had been out.

It was daylight but I couldn't hear anyone outside. I said, "Hey, anyone out there?" My voice was hoarse, but at least I could speak.

A man appeared I had never seen before. He was an older man with long gray hair. From his features I took him for an Indian. He had a doctor's stethoscope hanging from his neck.

He said, "Welcome back, Dirk, you came awfully close to leaving us these past few days."

I asked, "Who are you?"

"Well," he said, "I'm a friend of Jenny's, who is returning one of many favors owed. I'm a doctor and she asked me to come and have a look at you. You can thank her for being alive because she did everything right, and had you on the road to recovery before I got here.

"Now, if you'll sit up and take a few deep breaths, I would like to listen to your lungs." He listened with his stethoscope while I inhaled and exhaled several times. He said, "Well, your lungs are about cleared up and your fever is gone. I'll leave you in Jenny's capable hands. As usual, I'm needed elsewhere."

I thanked him as he shook my hand and left. I could hear people talking outside and as I was trying to get up, Jenny appeared.

"Dirk, you stay in that bed," and she pushed me back down. She said, "The doctor wants you to stay in bed another couple days, and I'm here to see you do it."

I said, "OK Jenny, and I want to thank you for pulling me through. The doctor told me I wouldn't be here if it wasn't for you and your native skills."

"Dirk," she replied, "There are few enough people left on this planet. I was happy to save one of the good ones. Now you rest and I'll bring you some good warm soup. You haven't eaten in almost three days."

She returned with the hot soup and Jeb. He helped me to sit up and Jenny spoon fed me the soup. I could have fed myself but I could see she wanted to, so I let her do it.

That was the best damned soup I ever recall eating. When I inquired as to the contents, Jeb laughed and said, "Dirk, I recall telling you before, never ask what she puts in anything. Just enjoy it because it's always good."

I found out the next day that I was unconscious when they had gotten me to the island. Jenny had force fed me things I had never heard of and warmed my bed with heated stones. It had done the job.

The old Indian was a friend of Jenny's who she said was training some of the younger Indians in medicine. There wasn't any modern medicine of any kind left so he was teaching them about the different things that could be found in nature to treat illness. Also he was instructing them on setting broken bones and even doing operations. Jenny thought of the man as a hero for her people.

I asked if my things were around and she had Jeb bring in my pack and my guns. He had cleaned and oiled my .270 rifle and my .22 automatic. I checked the handgun and slipped it under my pillow.

I dug into my backpack and found the books I had brought him. I told him that I hoped he liked mysteries and gave him three. *Honor Among Thieves* by Jeffrey Archer, *Rules of Evidence* by Jay Brandon, and *One Police Plaza* that I told Jeb was written by one of my favorite authors, William Caunitz. I told him I was sorry they were all mysteries but that was about all I had left in my meager library back at my cabin.

He was overjoyed. He said, "Dirk, thank you. Don't worry about them being mysteries. Diversity is great when it comes to reading. I will learn from them as I do from any book that I read. I used to keep something in my desk when I taught college classes that I read to the students on their first day. I don't think I ever knew the author but it was something that I came to believe. I'll recite it to you from memory and we'll see if you agree."

"There is divine beauty in learning, just as there is human beauty in tolerance. To learn means to accept the postulate that life did not begin at my birth. Others have been here before me and I walk in their footsteps. The books I have read were composed by generations of fathers and sons, mothers and daughters, teachers and disciples. I am the sum total of their experiences, their quests, and so are you."

As Jeb spoke I could see or I should say feel how those new college students must have felt. Almost like some higher being was addressing them. I was silent for a moment, thinking of something brilliant to say, but could only come up with, "Jeb, I have never heard anything close to that to explain the concept of learning. Yes, I agree with you."

He then told me how I had scared him when I was delirious and talking crazy in my sleep.

A feeling of dread rushed over me. I prayed I hadn't said anything about Calvin being a killer. I tried to appear casual and asked Jeb what it was I had talked about.

He said, "Well, you repeatedly said, 'I'll get them, Davey, I'll get them.'"

I asked him if he remembered anything else I had said. He thought a minute and said, "Yes, a couple of times you mentioned someone called Big George. I couldn't make out what you were talking about most of the time."

With that he told me he could see I was sleepy from the warm soup and said good night and left me to rest. After he left my mind was racing. Thank God I hadn't mentioned Cal in my sleep or anything about meeting the Bar-Track man. Calvin would have killed me in my sleep and the truth would never have been known. I needed to bide my time until I had my health back before I confronted Cal. I had to have the edge.

The change over the next three days was hard to believe. The first thing I did when I really felt like my old self was to heat up a couple of buckets of water and take a good bath. Jenny's cooking had my strength and energy back to normal. I must have lost twenty pounds when I was sick and the fact that I didn't carry any extra weight to begin with left me pretty slim.

I returned to my evening fireside chats with Jeb. He had found the last episode of quakes alarming. I told him about seeing the orange glow off to the northeast and he told me he had also seen it. He had figured it to have been an eruption somewhere close to the town of Silver Bay. That was a town on the north shore of Lake Superior.

He told me of how their winter had gone. He said either the fishing had gotten better then in previous winters or they had just located better spots to fish. Whatever the reason for it, fishing had been excellent all winter. They had eaten well.

When we got around to my turn to tell about how my winter had been, I told Jeb about meeting the boy whose name I had called out when I was sick. About how I had helped the boy and his mother prepare for the coming winter. I told him about the fun I had teaching the boy to hunt and fish.

Jeb said, "I sure would like to meet this lad. Dirk, you should bring him with you the next time you come."

I just went ahead and told him about how I had mentioned that to the boy and his mother. I even said, "I figured you would enjoy tutoring the boy and improve his education."

I told of how the boy had shot his first deer and how we had tracked it down. Also about how the boy worried about his mother's mental state. That kind of led me into telling about the boy's dad disappearing and my finding his body in that hole. At that point, Jeb said, "It sounds like you and that boy are real close." Jeb couldn't help but notice the expression on my face when I turned to him in the firelight and said, "We were Jeb, we were."

He had picked up the past tense in my words and he looked over at me not knowing what he should say. I said quietly, "In time, Jeb, you will know it all. I just need a few more days to get ready."

"I won't press it," he said. "But I sure have a bad feeling." He told me to sleep well, and headed for his tent.

After the fire died down I crawled into my sleeping bag and dozed off watching the little darting flames among the embers of the fire. I dreamt of standing on the shore of a little lake and watching a cabin burn. Watching it burn and consume the bodies of two people. Two people I had come to care about a great deal and now missed.

The next three days were spent fishing with Jeb. Walleye fishing was always the best in the month of May before the quakes had come and it still was. We had a great time but were also careful to put back any females that looked like they still held any spawn. We found the crappies were in full spawn in about four to five feet of water but we didn't keep any of those.

We worked the shallows around the islands and off the points. For the most part Jeb handled the lines while I provided the slow troll with an old set of oars and a lot of muscle. The fresh air, good diet and exercise had me back in great physical shape.

As we moved along the shore and around the islands, I watched the trees finish leafing out with birds starting to build their nests among the branches. I couldn't help but feel life was truly back to normal, at least as far a nature was concerned. Life for mankind would never be normal again, at least not until the generations that come re-established what they would come to consider normalcy.

Chapter 18

Jenny and Calvin left every morning to work in a garden they were preparing for planting somewhere in the area. Jenny was real excited about some tomatoes she had discovered in an old garden last summer. They had seeded themselves back every year in the unattended garden and Jenny had saved some of the dried seeds over the winter. She had managed to get some of them to sprout in some potted soil and was anxious to transplant them in the garden that her and Calvin were getting ready.

Just the thought of tomatoes brought back visions of B.L.T.s. They always were what I looked forward to every summer. I hadn't had one in many years now. In Minnesota, a home-grown tomato tasted like no other. The weather stayed nice and I was nearly my old self. Jeb even commented about me getting my strength back. He even made a little joke about taking up water skiing with me supplying the power.

Jeb and I decided to surprise Jenny with a grilled walleye supper. Her and Cal had been working in their garden until dusk for several nights and we knew she was tired when she got back to the island. Still having to fix supper is something I'm sure she didn't look forward to. We thought it would be a nice surprise.

When we saw them launching the boat to come back to the

island, Jeb put the walleye fillets on the grate over the hot coals. When they reached the island they were about ready to eat. Jenny was absolutely delighted with our little surprise.

Calvin appeared to be in a surly mood and said very little. After supper he made a remark about if I was so healthy again, maybe I should be putting some time in the garden, instead of fishing all day. Jeb told him I had worked all day rowing the boat, and reminded him that he was filling his belly with fish we had worked hard to get. Jeb was more upset then I was.

I didn't say anything because I didn't want to upset Jenny, but his rude remark made up my mind for me. Tonight was going to be the night. I figured out how I would set it up, and have a little surprise for Calvin. A little edge.

After supper, Jeb and I took up our usual positions by the fire. My normal spot was directly across the fire from Cal and Jenny's tent. I liked to sit low on a boat cushion with my back against a log. This allowed me to stretch my legs out toward the fire and relax. I kept my rolled up sleeping bag behind the log, and my right shoulder. I liked sleeping outside here by the fire, but when it rained I slept in Jeb's tent. Jeb had an old padded chair he liked to sit in. He sat down in it to my left as he usually did.

As we sat there, we were listening to an apparent argument Jenny and Cal were having in the tent. It had started out in low whispers but it was steadily getting louder. Apparently some Indian friends of Jenny's had passed by the garden that Cal and Jenny were working in. It seems Calvin had made some off-color remarks to a young Indian girl, and her father and Cal had some words. Jenny was reminding him that this wasn't the first time something like this had happened.

Cal told her he didn't much care what she thought because they were only Indians. That brought a moment of stunned silence from Jenny. Calvin came out of the tent and stood across the fire from me. He had an ugly scowl on his face and exclaimed, "Damn Indian bitch!"

I had my fill. I said, "Say Calvin, I forgot to tell you, I met up with your old friend."

Cal said, "Who the hell was that?"

I said, "The Bar-Track man." As soon as he heard me say it, the expression on his face changed.

His hands came out of his pockets, and he straightened up looking at me across the fire. He wasn't armed but I knew about the loaded rifle he kept just inside the tent.

"Well," he said, "Did you shoot that bastard like I told you to?"

I couldn't help but smile, when I said, "Oh yes, I killed him, and a friend of his. Your worries are over."

He just stood there, but from the expression on his face, I knew his mind was racing. I saw Jeb move away a few steps out of the corner of my eye.

"What the hell are you talking about?" Calvin asked. "That son of a bitch never worried me." He was getting worked up and talking very loud now.

"Oh, I think you've been worried about him for a long time. You see Cal, we had time for quite a talk before he died. One thing about me Cal, I'll always believe a dying man. It seems that his story about the rape and murder of Jenny's daughter differs a whole lot from yours."

"What's he mean, Cal?" Jenny asked, as she came out of the tent behind him.

It was the final showdown and Cal knew it. I noticed him turning toward the tent opening as he said, "I don't know what the hell he's talking about. Ask him, not me."

She turned to me and said, "What did that man tell you, Dirk?"

"Jenny," I said, "It seems he stumbled on Cal, just as he was covering your daughter's body. They saw each other about the same time, and Cal saw the opportunity to hang the girl's death on him. Only thing was, he missed him and let him get away. That's why he tells everyone to shoot him on sight. Cal didn't want the truth to ever get out."

Jeb spoke from the edge of the firelight, "I knew that girl was driving you nuts. I caught you watching her lots of times, if she went in swimming or took a bath. I never did feel right about that story you told us, about how that guy with the bad leg killed her."

"He's a liar," Cal screamed as he rushed into the tent. He reappeared almost instantly with a rifle he was leveling at me.

I was ready. I had been sitting with my right arm over the log behind me with my hand resting on the top of my rolled up sleeping bag. My hand came out of the middle of the rolled bag with my .22 automatic. I fired an instant before he did. I hit him and it threw him off just enough so his bullet just grazed my left cheek.

My bullet had hit him in the throat, and he was levering in another round as I fired twice. The first one hit below his left eye, the second just about in the center of his forehead. He dropped the rifle as he slumped to his knees. I heard him let out a long sigh, then he fell forward. I knew he was dead before he hit the ground.

All was quiet and Jenny kind of slowly sank to the ground. She was crying softly, kneeling there on the ground, not saying anything. Jeb walked over to her, helped her up and took her into the tent. I heard him tell her, "Now we know the truth Jenny, now she can rest in peace and Calvin has paid for his sins."

He came out of the tent and said, "She's going to be all right. She just needs some rest and time to come to terms with this." He walked over and looked at my cheek. The bullet had dug a furrow across my cheek. I could feel the blood soaking down my side inside my shirt.

Jeb said, "I'll get something to clean that up," and went into his tent. He returned with a pan of water and some towels to clean the wound. It was in a spot that was hard to bandage so he had me hold a compress that had some kind of disinfectant on it against the wound until it stopped bleeding. I got up and walked down to the water and washed the rest of the blood off me. I left my shirt in the water anchored with a rock to soak the blood out. I went back to the fire and dug a fresh shirt out of my pack and put it on. The wound had started to bleed a little again so I sat by the fire holding the compress against it.

Jeb came over and sat down. "How's the cheek?" he asked.

"I think it's going to be all right, if I can keep it clean until it scabs over," I replied.

"Damnedest thing I have ever seen," he said. "You sure were fast with that handgun. I can't help but wonder what the hell would have happened if Cal would have killed you."

I said, "I suspect he would have had to kill the both of you. He knew you both believed me, and Jenny would go to the Indians for help if he let her live."

Jeb said, "I believe you're right. I guess we never knew how evil he really was."

We rolled Calvin up in a blanket, and put him in the boat. In the morning we would take him to shore to bury him. I had suggested weighting him down with rocks, and sinking him in one of the deep holes in the lake. Jeb wouldn't hear of it. He said he would never be able to eat another fish from the lake if Cal was down there.

Later, as we sat by the fire, Jeb asked me, "Dirk, have you thought about what you're going to do now? Jenny and I would sure like to have you stay on here with us. I don't believe I could make it alone, as far as providing fresh meat. Oh, I always have done most of the fishing, but Cal did all the hunting. I guess what

I'm admitting here is, I'm getting a little too old to be dragging a deer any distance anymore."

I said, "Jeb, let's wait and talk about that in a day or two. I haven't really made any plans other then the one I had when I came back here. That one has been taken care of, so I guess I'll just sleep on making any other plans for a night or two. Besides, I think we better include Jenny when we talk about making plans for the future."

Jeb said, "You're right, we'll talk tomorrow. Get some rest."

Chapter 19

I added some wood to the fire and snacked on some pieces of fish that were left from supper, still warm in the pan. As I ate, I sat there and listened to the sounds of the night.

There will never be any music written that will equal the beauty of the sounds around a wilderness lake at night.

The haunting call of the loons. The rustling of leaves, moved by the soft evening breeze. The faint hooting of an owl from a nearby island, barely audible, due to the soft lapping of the waves against the shoreline rocks.

A feeling of peace and serenity washed over me as I lay back on my sleeping bag. I looked up at the half-moon and watched it play hide and seek with the small puffy clouds as they made their way across the night sky. I slept.

Jenny woke me, with the morning sun filtering through the trees behind her. She asked, "Are you hungry Dirk?"

I said, "Jenny, I'm starved. And a good morning to you. I sure hope you're feeling better this morning."

"I'm fine, Dirk," she said, "I guess it was just the shock of learning the truth. I can't believe I lived all these years with the man and never really knew what he was. I know you're not the kind of man who enjoys hurting other people. What you did, you did for Jeb and me. I thank you."

After breakfast Jeb and I loaded Calvin's body into the boat. Jenny went with us, but when we hit shore she said she was going to visit the Indians. She asked us not to mark the grave because she never wanted to know where he was buried. She said she might spend the night with her Indian friends and would light a fire in the usual spot to let us know when to come and get her with the boat.

We buried Cal and covered his grave with rocks and brush. No one would ever know where he was buried. While we were working I asked Jeb why Jenny was going to see the Indians. He didn't know.

We passed the day fishing and as usual I provided the oar power. I didn't mind because the weather was nice and I always enjoyed listening to Jeb talk. We quit when we had plenty for supper which Jeb volunteered to cook.

Jenny returned the following afternoon. We picked her up and as usual she had some goodies for us. The Indians had sent along some of Jeb's favorite jam that he loved to spread on Jenny's rice cakes. For me there was a beautiful deerskin shirt. Jenny had told them what had happened on the island and they were happy I had saved their friend Jenny from harm. The shirt was soft and fit perfectly. My shirt supply was really hurting so it sure was nice to get.

After we had returned to the island and had our supper, Jenny told me that her and Jeb had something to discuss with me. She said, "Dirk, are you planning to stay on here with us?"

I said, "Jenny, I think you're going to need me around. Jeb here is a good man, but getting along in years. He's going to need my help putting game on the table. When rice and maple syrup harvest time comes, you're going to need some help."

"Dirk, you don't have to stay unless you want to," Jenny said.

"I've told Jeb about a proposal the Indians have offered us. Jeb, why don't you tell Dirk about it?"

Jeb said, "The Indians want us to come and live with them. The doctor wants Jenny to work with him in the clinic. He just can't handle all the work by himself anymore. Also, they want me to teach their children. They don't have a really qualified teacher, so they want me to come and start a school."

Jenny said, "In exchange for our work, we will be compensated with a nice cabin, firewood, and food. During rice and syrup harvest times the school will be closed and everyone, including Jeb and I will help in the harvest."

Jeb said, "Dirk, we are indebted to you for our very lives. Please don't think we are deserting you. The Indians know how you saved Jenny and they want you to know that you are welcome to come and live among them."

I sat and thought for awhile. "Well," I said, "I've lived alone for years now. I believe it's become my way of life – not that I haven't enjoyed the time I've spent with you folks here on the island. My other contact with people ended in four deaths. Two were by my own hand, although I feel they were justifiable homicides.

"The other two," I continued, "were two people I let get inside of me. Two people I will think about forever. I don't care to get that close to anyone again. In this new world we find ourselves in, life isn't anything you can count on. I guess what I'm saying is, I'm going my own way.

"Jenny," I said, "I think your moving in with your people is a great idea. You are a caring person and you will enjoy working at the clinic. Jeb, there probably isn't a more qualified man to fill that teaching job left in the state. Hell, as far as we know, maybe in the whole damn country. The thing that will make it work is, you love to teach."

I said, "There is something I would like to see you do while you're teaching those young people. I realize that formal education is important, but learning about life and how to live it is even more important. Jeb, every once in awhile, slip in a little talk about how to treat other people, how to live in peace and harmony. Maybe we have a chance here. A chance to start this new world out right. If we do it right maybe the future generations that come from these survivors will have no need for prisons. No need for police or armies.

"Well," I said, "Now, we come to what I'm going to do. I have been wondering for years about what is really left of this country. I believe it's time for me to find out. I recall from those last radio broadcasts that I was able to pick up, that the southwest was under the ocean. I surely would like to see that and I believe I'm going to. I'll tell you what. I'll see you two get moved and settled in. Then with at least four good months of traveling weather left, I will head for Arizona. How does that sound?"

Jeb said, "Dirk, I wish I was young enough to go with you, but I'm not. My place is here with Jenny and her people. I know I have something that those children need – knowledge – and I'll do my best to see they get it. I do agree with you about teaching them to live in harmony and peace. I'll try to instill some of that in their daily schooling.

"Dirk," he said. "There is something I want you to know. We will never forget you. You don't know it but I've been writing a book since the quakes and eruptions started. You have become a big part of that book. I know you keep a daily journal and if you don't mind I would like to read it before you leave. When future generations read my book, I want them to know about all the things you did to correct some of the wrongs and help this new world off on the right start. These children will read about you and hopefully their children. I think it's very important that we all remember who Dirk Volcots really was."

I thought about it for a minute then said, "Sure you can have my journal. I've recorded my daily life since this whole mess started, but I don't think you will find much worth writing about in it. If you really want it, it's yours."

Jenny said, "Nonsense, Dirk. I'll bet that thing is full of interesting things. I would love to read it myself if that is all right with you."

I said, "You can read it if you like, but I have to tell you the first couple of years is pretty repetitive stuff."

She replied, "Dirk, I know that journal will show whoever reads it just how much good you have done. It will show how you have made an effort to do exactly as you say, about starting this new world out in the right way. We know you have corrected a lot of wrong and evil. I think Jeb's book is a good way of letting people know what you have done. Like Jeb said, you should be remembered."

"Well," I said, "That is going to be something. Me being part of a book. Jeb, I would like very much for you to mention someone else in that book. The man who revealed Calvin for what he was. A man who lived in fear of his life because of a killing he witnessed. A man whose life I took without ever even knowing his name."

Jeb interrupted me. "Dirk, put your mind at ease. All who read my book will know about him. And I felt it only fitting that they know him as you did. Simply as the Bar-Track man."

Chapter 20

Jeb and Jenny were all settled in their new cabin. It was all that had been promised by the Indians and more. Jenny was thrilled to have new curtains and a big picture window looking out over a beautiful meadow. A small stream ran down the meadow and it was filled with large rocks that made the stream give off gurgling sounds that could be heard in the cabin at night. Sounds that relaxed you, and made you feel at peace.

The Indians had provided a good supply of food and more then enough firewood. Jeb seemed more relaxed then I had ever seen him. He had been worried about providing for Jenny, had she not taken the Indians up on their offer. He was nearly giddy about being able to teach again. He told about how he had planned to divide his students by age, and the curriculum he had set up for each age group.

The Indian elders had informed him that nineteen students would be attending the new school. They would range from six to fifteen years of age. The ones older than fifteen had attended school for at least five years and therefore had at least a basic education before the quakes hit. Also, they were needed for hunting and gathering food for the tribe.

Teaching materials were a problem. Every abandoned house

and cabin for miles around were searched for books, paper, maps and anything else that could be put to use in a school.

Jeb ended up with quite an assortment. Someone even came up with a chalkboard and a sizable supply of chalk. It was mounted on the wall behind Jeb's desk in his new schoolhouse. The school was actually an old fire barn used by the area volunteer fire department prior to the quakes. Tables and chairs had been brought in and a large wood burning stove was installed in one corner. Two Indians that had worked previously as carpenters had installed large windows to let in all the light they could. With no electrical power, lighting a large room was a problem. The big windows that had been taken from some lake cabins proved more than adequate.

With Jenny and Jeb settled in their new cabin and Jeb's school about ready to open, I decided it was time for me to leave for the southwest as I had planned. It was nearing mid summer and I wanted to be well south of the winter weather before it became too severe.

As we sat around after supper that next evening, I told Jenny and Jeb that I planned to be on my way at first light in the morning. They both begged me to stay on but soon realized my mind was set and I wouldn't be deterred.

Jenny started gathering things she insisted I take along, and somehow found room to squeeze them into my backpack. I told her it was going to be pretty heavy to carry, but she just laughed and told me it would get lighter each day as I ate my way through the things she had packed for me.

At bedtime, Jenny had tears in her eyes as she wished me the best of luck. She said, "Dirk, if anyone survived in the desert southwest, it would be Indians. The high country of northeast Arizona may still be intact. That area was populated mostly by Indians, Navajo and Hopi reservation land covers most of the

Arizona high country in the northeast quarter of the state. I'm sure they would help you if you need it. They know how to survive in hard times so I would bet they are still there."

I told Jenny I would look for Indians if I needed help and she went off to bed.

Jeb said, "I will be up in the morning to see you off," and headed for bed also.

I laid on the couch for hours before I slept, thinking about what and who I was leaving behind. I was comfortable leaving now, knowing the people I cared about were safe and provided for. I would miss them but I knew if I was going to see what was left of this country, I had to get started now before age caught up to me. Maybe I would return here in time to come. It would be a comfortable place to end my years.

Jeb, true to his word, was up when I was ready to leave. He said, "I have a small going-away present for you." He handed me a book, a diary that had never been used. He said, "I made an entry inside the front cover. It's something that's long been a favorite of mine. Every time I think of it, you come to mind. It comes from the diary of Henry David Thoreau. I believe he wrote it sometime in the mid-eighteen hundreds. Read it tonight and other nights by your evening fire and remember us."

I took the book and clasped the man's hand. I told him, "Jeb, there will never be a day in my life that I will not have thoughts of you and Jenny. Don't be surprised if I appear again at your fire sometime down the road."

Jeb smiled at that as he remembered the first time he met me. It was the morning they found me asleep beside the fire out on their island. So much had happened since then. He helped me with my pack and we shook hands, wishing each other luck. I told him to give Jenny a hug for me, picked up my rifle and headed out.

Jeb had supplied me with maps of every state I was likely to pass through. Those and my two compasses should keep me from getting lost. I guess I really didn't care if I did get lost, as long as I held a southwest direction and beat the coming winter.

I planned to stay clear of all cities. I figured any survivors left in the cities survived by taking from others, and they wouldn't hesitate to take from me. Despite the heavy pack and having to work my way around a lot of tangled vegetation and crevices in the ground, I figured I had maybe covered a little better then twenty miles when it was time to look for a good spot to camp for the night. I had walked straight south. My intent was to hit a road that would take me a little west to a small community called Pike Lake. There I would again head south on a road I knew that would take me around the city of Duluth. Also, that road would keep me on high ground for a good two more days travel south. At least it used to be high ground when I last drove it.

The day had passed without my seeing another person, or for that matter, even a sign of another human. I did see some game, but with all the food Jenny had loaded me down with, there was no need for me to shoot anything. I found a good spot to camp just off the road and slid the pack to the ground. My first steps without the weight felt like I could jump six feet high. What a relief.

I soon has a small fire going and water boiling for wild rice and pieces of browned venison I stirred in. When it was ready I sat back and thought about my day while I ate.

I had first walked past cabins, and then many homes. Even a few small farms. They had all been overgrown with vegetation and some had already fallen apart. I couldn't help but notice a few of them had bullet holes in and around the windows. Just about all of them showed signs of being ransacked on more then several occasions.

After supper I opened my new diary and read what Jeb had

written on the inside of the cover:

"Denuded pines stand in
the clearings with no old
cloak to wrap about them,
only the apexes of their
cones entire, telling a
pathetic story of the
companions that clothed
them. So stands a man. His
clearing around him, he
has no companions on the
hills. The lonely traveler,
looking up, wonders why he
was left when his companions
were taken."

May god be with you every day of your journey. Dirk, you are in our prayers. Return to us.

Your Friend Always

Jebula Sandburg

I read the passage over several times. I could see how it had made Jeb think of me. Tomorrow on the trail I would memorize it. It would be something I would be able to recall whenever I thought of what I had left behind. It gave me a warm feeling to know I had friends to return to, like a family.

Chapter 21

Two days later found me well south of the city of Duluth. I was on the edge of a high ridge and could see a long ways to the south and east. Jeb had been right in predicting I would find the lower elevations covered with water. All the lower land before me was flooded. The high land that I stood on ran to the west and northwest. Lake Superior, that the city of Duluth was located on, had an elevation of 600 feet prior to the quakes. All the land to the west and north of the lake ran up to anywhere from 1,000 to 2,000 feet above sea level. Most of the land to the south along the Minnesota and Wisconsin border ran well below 1,000 feet.

Jeb's theory was that the oceans had risen and flooded the land to around the 1,000 foot mark. This I knew probably was true from the reports of cities being flooded before communications were lost after the quakes. Seeing that there was no way I could continue south, I turned to the southwest. The ground there according to the Minnesota map that Jeb had provided me, stayed for the most part above the 1,000 foot level.

I figured to pass to the north of Mille Lacs lake, to the southwest of where I was. The map showed the lake itself with an elevation of 1,250 feet. Then I would head for the southwest corner of Minnesota. That would keep me on good high ground until I hit the so-called “Buffalo Ridge.”

This ridge of high ground ran across the southwestern corner of Minnesota from the South Dakota border. South of this ridge water drained to the south towards the Missouri River. North of the ridge water ran northeast towards the Minnesota River. Elevations along this ridge were as high as 1,700 feet in the very southwest corner of Minnesota where the four states of Minnesota, Iowa, South Dakota, and Nebraska met.

The weather continued to cooperate. I had put up with only one heavy rain since starting out. The temperatures were staying in a real comfortable range that I guessed to be the upper sixties, and the nights had been nearly perfect for good sleeping.

The road I was now on was better then any I had traveled so far. There were many places I could stay walking on the road itself for a mile or more before having to skirt around a crevice or giant heaves that pushed the blacktop surface high in the air. Old road signs told me I was on the road I wanted to be on. It was number 210 that ran almost straight west before curving southwest after passing about fourteen miles north of Mille Lacs lake.

Still no sign of anyone alive. My pack was now lighter and I started to keep an eye out for game. Waterfowl were abundant and fairly easy to approach. I knew it wouldn’t be long before they bunched up and headed south for the winter.

It took me sixteen days to reach the town of Pipestone, about eight miles from the South Dakota border. I found a small stream just south of the abandoned town and made my camp for the night. I found an old sign that said I was on Split Rock Creek.

By the firelight, I went over my maps. I calculated I had covered about 340 miles. My average was only 21 miles a day. Hopefully, when I hit the flatter country that I knew lay ahead, my daily average would improve. Before sleep came that night a little depression crept in. The fact that I had not seen any sign of life was bothering me. It felt good inside knowing I had people to go back to. As always, I made my daily entry in my journal. I wrote of how the land I passed through was returning to nature. Even the wildlife around me seemed to look at me in wonderment. Most of them having been born after the quakes, had never seen a man. God's earth was truly renewing itself.

I plotted my course for the next few days travel. To avoid passing too close to the town of Sioux Falls to my west, I would head south into Iowa for about 25 miles. There I would take a road numbered eighteen that ran west, but only passed through very small towns. It also passed over the Missouri River. I hoped I would find the bridge still intact over the river when I got there. From there I could angle off and follow a road numbered 183 across Nebraska. It appeared the best route that avoided large towns.

I didn't want to follow any of the large freeways because they went through all the major cities. My last objective was highway number 40. That would take me into the northern Arizona high country.

Soon after starting out the next morning I noticed an irregular gray line along the horizon to the south. Each hour I walked made it a little more distinct, but I knew it was a long way off. I figured I would be heading west before I ever reached it or got close enough to figure out what it was.

That night I camped near the town of Canton in South Dakota. I set up camp on the west side of a small stream that was called the Big Sioux river. It had been a very good day with sunny skies and a cooling breeze, I figured from my map that I had covered about thirty miles.

It was just after dark when I was startled by the whinny of a horse. I sat up, tense, my mind racing. It had come from downstream, and fairly close. I was sure it was from my side of the river. I listened for a long time desperately hoping to hear it again. All I heard were the usual night sounds. Due to overcast skies, the night was too dark to go wandering about in the wooded stream bed looking for a horse.

I started to plan for morning. The horse had probably come to the stream for water. I could do nothing but wait for morning and pick up its tracks. Chances are it would be very wild and there was a good chance it had never seen a man before. Somehow I was going to have to come up with some rope or wire to catch it with.

Having been around horses for years while I was growing up was going to be a big help. One thing bothering me was the fact that the horse had whinnied. Normally, they didn't do that unless they saw another horse or a person they were familiar with. Maybe that was it. Someone had ridden him or had led him to water.

I slept little that night and broke camp at the crack of dawn. I was excited, yet knew I had to be very cautious. If someone was with that horse, he was a survivor. He also would be very wary.

It was hard to stay in cover and search for tracks along the stream bank. I had traveled close to a mile when I saw the tracks. There hadn't been one horse, there had been three. Also, I had been right in thinking there could have been a rider. He had left moccasin-type tracks along the stream. I figured they were moccasins because the edges of the tracks were curved and there was no distinctive break between the heel and the souls of his feet.

The tracks were slightly longer then mine but I noticed my track went deeper into the soil then his. Also he seemed to take a very long stride. I judged him to be very tall and slim. I found where he had camped near the stream and where he had headed west when he had left. I figured he had started out less than an hour before I found his camp. The horses were walking in a straight line so he must have them tied together with long lead ropes. They were walking.

I adjusted my pack and set out after them. They were headed in the direction I wanted to go, and I wanted one of those horses so bad I could taste it. I thought of how I could increase the miles I covered every day with a good horse under me, especially with the open plains ahead of me. Also, it would greatly improve my chances of survival if I was spotted and pursued in the open country ahead.

As I walked I checked my map and found there was a highway running north and south maybe seven miles ahead. It was the road I had planned to take south to catch another road west that crossed the Missouri river. The river was still nearly 80 miles away, but if I had that horse I could cover that in about half the time it would take walking. I tried to come up with a plan to use when I caught up to the horseman. No telling how he will react so I would just have to handle whatever happens.

About two hours later I saw the highway ahead of me. I crawled up the bank to the road. I looked north and it was a mess. Huge slabs of concrete were twisted up in all directions about a half a mile away. Looking south, I saw the rider and the horses. There were three horses and they were about a mile away walking along the west side of the road. I figured he was thinking of turning west somewhere ahead. According to my map the next road to the west was the one I had planned to take, number 18.

My problem now was if he looked back he was sure to see me. I had to let him get well ahead of me. If he did spot me he would take off and I would never see him again. Then my hopes of having a horse would be gone.

When he was nearly out of sight I started after him. I kept the same distance, but had to set a grueling pace to keep him in sight. I found myself hoping he would stop and take a break of some kind, but he never did. I did see him pull the horse with the pack on up to him and take something out of the pack which he ate, but he never got off his horse.

It was dusk and I was about ready to give it up when he stopped. He dismounted and pulled the saddle and pack off the horses. He was at a cross road and he led the horses to a water filled ditch and let them drink. By now I was close enough to see him tie something between the front legs of the horses. I recalled reading of how they did that in the west to keep the animals from straying far from their camp. I believe they were called hobbles.

The tall man then walked back to his saddle and pack. He carried them into a small grove of trees. I waited until I could see the glow of a fire he had started and decided it was now or never. Walking directly towards his fire, I called out, "Hello, I'm coming in slow and peaceful."

As I passed the tree line, a voice startled me. It said, "You sure are one determined walking man." He was standing against a tree about twenty feet to my right. His thumbs were hooked in over his belt with his jacket open. I saw no weapon.

I was carrying my .270 in the crook of my left arm. I stopped and started to turn toward him.

When I moved he said, "If you try to use that rifle, I will kill you. I mean that, and mister, you have no chance."

I stood and looked him over in the fading light. He stood at least six foot four. He wore a dark cowboy hat that covered shoulder-length light brown, almost blond hair. The beard on his long face was trimmed. He was dressed in a deer skin jacket, dark pants, and cowboy boots. I guessed him to be somewhere in his mid-forties.

I said, "Mister, I mean you no harm. You're the first man I've seen in weeks of traveling and I would be proud to share what I have over your fire. That is if you would like some company. If not, I will be on my way."

He moved toward me, saying, "Walk on over to the fire and we'll talk on it."

His voice and demeanor were definitely western. As he approached, I could see the handle of a pistol in the opening of his jacket. The gun wasn't stuck in his waist band but appeared higher, like it was in a shoulder holster. The grip of the pistol was white, like maybe pearl.

When we got to the fire I said, "I've got some wild rice, smoked meat, and some other things."

He said, "Hell, I ain't had me some rice for years. I believe I'd enjoy some of that."

I got some water heating over the fire for the rice while I chopped up some meat to cook with it. As I fixed our supper he said nothing more but seemed to be studying me. He did fetch some wood and dug two metal plates and spoons out of his pack.

When he moved, he moved like a cat, smooth and fluid. I could see his eyes watching me. They were kind of a strange color, a real light gray. His facial features never seemed to change or show emotion in any way. When the meal was ready I filled a plate and handed it to him. I said, "What's your name?"

"Luke," he said, "Luke Bowdry."

I reached out my hand toward him and said, "Dirk Volcots. Pleased to make your acquaintance, Luke. Where are you from? Not around here from the sound of that accent."

He simply replied, "Nope," and kept on eating. After a few minutes he looked at me and said, "Damn fine chow. A man gets real tired of an all-meat diet after a time. Don't believe it to be good for a man neither."

I figured it was time to open up the conversation a little so I told him about where I had brought the rice from and how it was harvested in the fall.

After refilling his plate, he inquired if there were other people up there in northeastern Minnesota. I told him there were Indians and two friends of mine named Jenny and Jeb.

After we had finished our supper we cleaned our plates and settled down by the fire. I wanted to know more about this man so I asked him, "Where you headed for, Luke?"

"Oh," he replied, "I reckon in the general direction of what used to be home. Although if I find some place that feels right along the way, that'll be home."

He went on to tell me he had been north of Hankinson, North Dakota to look for his only relative, a brother who had a place there. He said he had found the place, but no sign of the brother or his family or any livestock.

He said, "I figured on heading back the way I had come before winter sets in. My brother used to brag on surviving the North Dakota winters. Never could figure why a man would be proud of such a thing."

"Where is it that you came from?" I asked.

"Had me a ranch near Green River, Utah," he said. "Nothing left there now though. Folks stole the stock then burned it."

I inquired if he had seen any people in his travels and he told me he had seen two men about a week ago up in North Dakota. Then he said, "It didn't work out."

From the way he said it, I figured he didn't want to talk about it, so I let it go. He then laid back on his sleeping bag and said, "You best get some rest. After that walkin you did today I'm surprised you ain't asleep on your feet." Then, almost like an afterthought, he said, "Dirk, where in hell are you headed for anyway?"

"Well, I'm just kind of seeing the country, or what's left of it.

I thought I would head down towards Phoenix and spend the winter in a warmer climate. I'm not getting any younger so I thought it's now or never."

Luke said, "Hell, from what I seen today you can still cover ground with the best I ever saw. As far as Arizona goes you're in for a disappointment."

I asked, "Why is that?"

"Cuz, most of it just blew up. Over a hundred of them mountains blew their tops and buried all the valleys and lowlands in twenty feet or more of ash and poison gases. Damn few folks survived, if any at all. Then I heard salt water came in from the south and covered half the state or what was left of it."

He offered no more and rolled on his side toward the fire. Fatigue overtook me and I slept with my mind filled with wonderment over what I had just been told.

Chapter 22

Over the morning fire Luke and I looked over my maps. Luke didn't own a map an claimed he didn't need one. We agreed to travel together and head toward his cabin that was somewhere northeast of the Grand Canyon in Utah.

Luke warned me that the last part of the trip would be the worst. He said there were no roads left and it would take days to cover a few miles of mountainous terrain.

With no saddle available, I rode Luke's spare horse. We tied my gear on the pack horse with Luke's. As we started out I asked Luke, "Has this horse got a name Luke?"

"Yeah," Luke said, "I call him horse." He then pulled out ahead of me with the pack horse in tow. Luke was not long on conversation.

We were headed in a general southwest direction. Twice we stopped to water the horses and stretch our legs. Luke never did talk a lot all day. If I made a comment about something I saw, he would just mumble a yes or nod his head to acknowledge he heard me.

It was late in the afternoon when I saw what looked like two men on a horse well out ahead of us. I said, "Damn Luke, looks like we got company."

Luke said, "Yeah, but the wrong kind. Those are the two I told you about last night." He then turned to me and said, "Stay out of it, Dirk, I'll handle it."

The way he had said to stay out of it was cold and serious. Nevertheless, I unbuttoned my coat to have access to my handgun.

We stopped when we were about twenty-five feet from the two men on the horse. They stopped when we did. I saw no gun on the man in the saddle but his coat was open. He was a large man, much bigger then the one sitting behind him. I saw the man behind him had a rifle resting crosswise in front of him. He had both hands on it. He was a small very thin man that looked very dirty. The hand I cold see on the rifle barrel was nearly black with dirt. He hadn't bathed in a long time.

The one on the rear of the horse spoke, "Well, we meet again. Only thing is this time you ain't got that big fancy handgun on us. I see you did give one of your spare horses to somebody."

Luke said, "I didn't give him to anybody. Fella was headed my way so I let him ride along. No damn business of yours what I do anyway."

The little man replied, "You told us to go to hell when we asked you for that horse, so now we'll take them all." With that he jumped back off the horse's rear, leveling the rifle toward us as he hit the ground. There were two shots fired. Fired so fast they almost sounded like one. My horse was going wild and with no saddle under me to hang onto, I slid off before getting thrown off.

The little man with the rifle was thrown backwards several feet when the big bullet hit him in the chest. His rifle flew up in the air. The big man in the saddle slowly slid off the horse, his empty hand coming out of his coat. He never had time to even reach the gun in his belt. Both men were dead when they hit the ground. Both had been shot in the chest.

Luke calmly ejected the two spent shells and reloaded. He pocketed the two casings. I didn't know what to say. I would never have believed that a man could draw and fire a handgun that fast and accurately had I not just seen it. Luke Bowdry was one hell of a dangerous man to mess with. That gun had appeared in Luke's hand so fast it was a blur.

Luke turned to me and said, "Well, you got yourself a saddle and a horse if you want him. He looks pretty well used up, but with some rest and good grass he'll come around."

He then dismounted and checked the two men. He put the little man's rifle on the pack horse and offered me the other man's pistol. It was an old .38 with only four bullets in it. We checked his pockets but there were no more. I stuck the gun in my pack.

Luke asked, "You want their boots or any of their clothes?"

I told him that I didn't want anything and switched the saddle from the big black horse the dead men had rode in on to the horse I had been riding.

"We'll ride on a ways before we camp," Luke said, "I don't feel like bedding down next to trash."

After supper I broke out my journal and started to bring it up to date. Luke asked me what I was doing and I told him about keeping a daily diary. He commented about how I had only written a few pages. I then told him about giving my last journal to Jeb back in Minnesota. I told him about the book that Jeb was going to write.

Luke laughed at that and said, "You must have had a damn exciting life to have a man want to write a whole damn book on you."

I then gave him a kind of back history about how I survived in my little cabin and how I had met up with people through the past years. I told him about a couple of men I had killed and why. It was getting late so I told him I would finish the story another time and we turned in.

The next morning Luke was real quiet again so I figured I'd get him to tell me a little about his past. I looked over at him as we rode along and asked, "Luke, where did you learn to handle a pistol like that?"

He said, "Growing up on a big ranch, guns were a part of life. All the men who worked on ranches owned pistols and we used to shoot a lot. More like something to do for amusement then anything else. Hell, I knew a couple of fellas back then were really quick, make me look really slow."

He went on, "Dirk, don't get the idea that I thought shooting those two scum back there was fun. Killing is never fun. Like I told you before, those two and me parted on unfriendly terms the last time we met. They wanted my horse but never got him. I told them then if I saw either one of them again, I wouldn't leave them standing."

"Well," I said, "You are a man of your word, and as you said, they had fair warning."

As we traveled to the west, our luck held. We found enough game to fill our needs and plenty of good grass for our horses. The weather stayed tolerable and with good horses under us we covered a lot of miles. Every day I appreciated having a good saddle under me and damn good company to pass the time with. I grew to believe I had been blessed with about the finest traveling companion a man could ask for. Like me, a true survivor.

After about a week, the big black horse, who much to Luke's chagrin I had nicknamed Smokey, improved a great deal. I started to ride him for a few hours for a couple of days, then rode him all the time. Unlike the animal I had been riding, he seemed to move with a fluid-like motion. I could sense the power in him.

I worked at getting Luke to open up a little more each day. I mentioned that I had seen him pocket his empty shell casings. He explained that he had reloading supplies at his cabin in the mountains. He had gathered a lot of it from abandoned sporting goods stores and gun shops after the quakes. He said guns and ammo were a big part of the west and every little town had stores that sold guns and shooting supplies.

We talked about guns and my .22 automatic. He had seen me shoot and expressed surprise at how accurate it was for an automatic. He told me to save the brass from my .270 because he was equipped to reload them. He said the .270 was one of the most popular calibers in the west.

It was great traveling with a good horse under me and a traveling companion to talk to about things and places I had never seen. We crossed the rolling plains of Nebraska for what seemed forever until finally one afternoon Luke pointed ahead to what he said was the start of the Rockies. Luke agreed with me about my policy of skirting around all cities and towns. He said he knew a way around Denver and drew it out that night by the fire. I could tell from the way he described it, I was in for a tough journey.

The next two weeks passed with little incident. We were now in mountainous country just south of Denver, Colorado. We camped on the bank of a small river. Luke said it was the South Platte and the next day we should run into a small town called Conifer. He said there we would hit a road numbered 285 that we could follow west. We had passed through some beautiful country. Luke said it used to be called the Pike National Forest.

The dust was a constant problem. It was kicked up by the horse's hooves and seemed to hang in the air. You could look back and see our dust hanging in the air a mile off.

That night I heard Luke get up to check the horses. They were jumpy but I just figured there was an animal in the area that they had smelled. I must have just dozed off when I was startled by Luke shaking my shoulder. He motioned for me to be quiet and come away from the fire. I pulled my boots on, holstered my handgun from under my pillow, picked up my rifle and followed him.

When we were out of the firelight, he said, "We ain't alone. Follow me, but don't make a sound."

I followed as quiet as I could through the trees and rocks. In about fifteen minutes we crawled out on a big flat boulder. About five hundred feet below us there was a small fire between some big rocks. There appeared to be three men sitting near the fire. They were talking and gesturing in what appeared to be our direction. Luke nudged me and pointed to the rocks above and behind the men. I saw nothing and shook my head.

Luke motioned for me to follow and we headed for our camp. When we got back to our camp, Luke pushed dirt over the dying coals with the side of his boot. "They know we're here," he said, "I got close enough earlier to hear them talking. They want our horses and plan to take them. The ones they have are in bad shape."

I asked, "When are they coming?"

"I didn't hear that part, but I figure early in the morning." Luke replied, "They won't let us get mounted and leave because their horses aren't in good enough shape to catch us."

"Well, it's your call, Luke. You have a hell of a lot more experience with this kind of thing. By the way, what were you pointing at up in those rocks back by their camp?"

He said, "The forth man. They're a pretty careful bunch to keep a man on watch out here where the odds are damn slim of ever seeing anybody. Then again, maybe they were just being careful cause we were here. Either way, they ain't still alive because they're dumb."

I said, "The way I see it, we could leave now or wait for them to come in the morning. What do you think, Luke?"

I could see Luke kind of smile in the dim moonlight. "No, I don't figure running is the way to go. Even with bad horses they would probably follow and jump us where we camp tomorrow night. I think our biggest problem is there are four of them against us two. How about if we surprise them real early in the morning? When they roll out we take two of them out with our first two shots. Then we got us even odds."

As first light broke, we were back on the flat rock overlooking their camp. Luke saw a better vantage point about two hundred feet to the left and a little lower. He moved down to it and waved when he was in position. We had agreed that when the last man started to make up his bedroll we would open up. It seemed like the most likely time that the four of them would be close together. Luke would take a man on the left, and I would take one to the right. That way we wouldn't both shoot the same man.

As the light improved I could see one of the bedrolls was still unoccupied. I searched the rocks but saw nothing. We had hoped to catch the four of them together. I even thought he may be off relieving himself, but minutes slipped by and he didn't return. I could hear the sounds of several horses but I couldn't see them from where I was. Maybe that was where the missing man was. I only hoped Luke could see him.

It was near full light before one of the men stirred. The man on the far left sat up and pulled on his boots. He said something I couldn't really hear a couple of times to his two sleeping companions and they finally started to get up.

I put the scope on my .270 on the man to the right. He was about average size with a long scraggly beard. His hair was long and black, tied back in a thick braid. I estimated he was about a hundred and fifty yards away but at a sharp downhill angle.

I watched the group through the scope and in a couple of minutes the man in the center picked up a rifle from the ground near his bedroll. He levered a round into the chamber. It appeared to be an old Winchester carbine with no scope.

The other two then started to check their hand guns. I couldn't see any other rifles, but no doubt the other man on watch would have one. For a few minutes I didn't think they were going to break camp before they came to jump us. Then the man in the middle knelt down and started to roll up his bedding.

It was cool but I had to wipe the sweat from my forehead. I wondered if this was bothering Luke like it was me. I had never shot a man without warning in my life. I had to remind myself what these men had in mind for us. Again, it came down to basic survival. I put my scope on the man that was mine and waited. I reminded myself to allow for the steep downhill angle. My mind kept going back to the forth man. Where the hell was he?

Luke's target was now picking up his bedroll, but mine just stood there talking. I glanced down at Luke. He was leaning against a big rock and was sighting his rifle toward the group of men below. He looked as steady as the rock he was leaning on. I was glad he was on my side.

Then I looked back at my man. He turned, bent down, and started to roll up his sleeping bag. My .270 rocked my shoulder back and the man pitched forward on his face.

Luke's shot was a split second behind mine. His man staggered back several steps, looked down at his blood-covered stomach and fell backwards.

I worked my bolt as quick as I could and got a shot off at the third man as he threw himself behind some cover. I didn't think that I had hit him.

The man then hollered out twice what sounded like, "Key, Key." No doubt the name of the missing forth man. I searched every crack and crevice I could see, but I couldn't find him.

I looked over for Luke but he had moved out of sight. No doubt he was moving down to get the man I had missed. I figured I had better move too because they probably knew where I was from the shots I had fired.

I was sliding back off the rock when it hit me. I felt the pain before I heard the shot. It was like nothing I had ever experienced before. A hot searing pain in my lower right back, just above my hip. I was shot clean through. It had come out just below my ribs. Blood was splattered all over the rock.

I made myself roll a few feet to some small rocks and scrub pine. I prayed he couldn't see me. Damn that forth man. I rolled up the bottom of my coat and pressed it against the wound on my right side trying to stop the flow of blood. It was bad. I heard two shots from below me and then quiet for a long time. I couldn't tell if it was Luke shooting or not. Damn that forth man. We should have waited until he joined the others when they were ready to come after us. Well, nothing I could do about it now, but lay here and hope Luke got lucky. I just wished there was some way for me to let him know I was out of it and he was on his own.

Strange how I lay here probably bleeding to death, yet had no thoughts about dying. I told myself I would survive. I pulled myself up into a sitting position and put the .270 across my knees. I opened the bolt and pushed two rounds down into the clip to replace the two I had fired. This was the old sportster model that loaded through the bolt opening. I looked around but saw nothing moving. I was glad I was now in the shadows and would be hard to see. At least the man who had shot me from behind wouldn't get another clean shot.

Then I heard someone shouting, "Get-get," and heard horses running. It had to have been Luke running off their horses. A minute later there was another shot. This time I was sure it was

Luke's big handgun. Someone said something, and it sounded like he was in agony. Then it was quiet again.

I checked my wound and the blood flow had slowed quite a bit. I knew if I didn't get some help or at least some water soon I would die. God, what I wouldn't give for some cool water. It seemed like the pain had decreased, but I was real tired.

I don't know how much time had passed because I had dozed off. My senses were still working because the sound of a man walking in loose gravel snapped me awake. Someone was moving down to where Luke had been when this thing got started. He was half sliding down the steep slope so he was making noise. About the time I couldn't hear him anymore there were three fast shots. The first and the last sounded like the same gun. I hoped it was Luke's.

All was quiet again and I must have dozed off when I heard the best sound I had heard in years. Luke was calling my name, "Dirk, Dirk, where the hell are you."

My voice was hoarse but I managed to get him to hear me calling to him. When his face appeared over the rocks all he said was, "Oh Christ." He laid me down and told me he would be right back.

Chapter 23

I woke up next to a warm fire. I could feel something had been wrapped tightly around my body. I looked around and it was snowing. I felt warm but it was snowing.

Across the fire Luke was sitting with a blanket over him snoring softly. I said, "Hell of a nurse you are, sleeping on the job."

He snapped awake and said, "About time you woke up."

Thirsty as hell, I said, "Luke, we got any water?"

"Sure," he said, and handed me a canteen. "Got that off them boys we tangled with. Damned if they didn't have some ammo for my handgun in one of their packs." He reached over and took the water away from me. "Too much of that will hurt you. I'll let you have a little more later."

I said, "What are we going to do Luke? I'm going to be laid up for some time."

"Well," he said, "I figure tomorrow we'll head downstream. I was there years ago and this river widens out into a lake. I believe it's called Cheesman Lake. Anyway, I recall there were cabins on it and I figure it will be a good place to winter and let you heal up. We should make it by mid-day and then you'll have a warm bed to sleep in."

I said, "You figure I can make a half a day's ride in my shape?"

"Dirk," he said, "You have to make it. Unless we get to good shelter you won't live more then a few days. I'm going to tie you on your horse. With any luck, you'll pass out until we get there."

Luke, true to his word, tied me on my horse and we headed out at daybreak. It was tough country and despite Luke's efforts to find the easiest trail the pain soon overwhelmed me. I woke up realizing Luke was helping me off my horse. I was only half conscious when I felt myself being undressed on what felt like a soft bed. I was having trouble focusing my eyes. I felt Luke cleaning my wounds with something soft and warm, then I slept.

I heard Luke calling my name. I opened my eyes and he was sitting by the bed. There was sunlight coming in the window over my bed. Luke said, "Dirk, try to eat some of this, and held some warm liquid up to my mouth with a large spoon. It was warm and tasted good. I let him feed me what was in the bowl and felt it start to warm my insides. I asked him what it was.

He said, "Broth made from boiled meat and bone marrow. It should help you get some strength back. You sure had me scared you weren't going to come out of it. You been out for two days. You better eat all you can now because you lost one hell of a lot of blood. I must have poured a quart out of that boot of yours when I pulled you off that horse. I got to say you are one tough man."

"How long we been here?" I asked.

"Just the two days you were out of it. Looks like I picked us a good place to winter. I shot a nice mule deer yesterday evening, that broth you just ate came from him. Anyway, we are set for meat for a good while, and from all the tracks I found down by that lake, food is not going to be any problem."

"Luke, what are my chances?" I asked him right out.

He studied on it for a minute, then he said, "Well, the fact you lived through the trip getting here, had a good rest and now some warm food is a damn good sign. I think if we keep that wound clean and infections don't set in or you come down with a fever you'll make it just fine. Infection is the thing to look out for. I'm boiling those pieces of sheet that I been using to wrap around your middle but that's about all I can do."

I said, "I sure want to thank you. I hate being a burden and not holding up my end. Luke, you will get paid back if it's the last thing I ever do."

He said, "Forget it Dirk. Now you get some rest and in a couple hours I will get you up again for some more food."

I did eat that night and again the following morning. Around noon things started to change. I began to run a fever and by nightfall I was sweating profusely.

Two days passed and the fever finally broke. I woke with a wet towel on my forehead. Again, the sun was shining in on me. For some reason I wanted to go out in the clean white snow, and breathe the cold clean air.

My back ached something fierce where the bullet went in. Where it had come out, below my right ribs, didn't bother me at all.

After a while Luke came in and I said, "How's the weather?"

"Well," he said, "He lives. Weather is just fine. Sunny and about forty above. Pretty typical Colorado winter day."

I said, "Damn pain in my back woke me up. It hurts like hell, but I believe I better have some chow."

Luke went about warming some food, and while it warmed over the fire I told him I would like to see outside. He pushed my bed over by the door so I could look out. It was a warm sunny day and the fresh air coming through the open door felt great.

The cabin was on a slope near the end of the lake where the river we had followed came in to the right. I could see the open water of the river through the pines where it entered the lake down the hill from the cabin. About a hundred yards out from where the river entered the lake it was frozen over from shore to shore. Tall snow covered pines surrounded the lake and extended up the mountain slopes in all directions.

I said, "Luke, this is one of the most beautiful places I believe I've ever seen."

"Yep," he said. "Thought so myself. Been thinking about pulling a boat I found by the next cabin down to that open water and try fishing."

I said, "You never told me you did any fishing."

"Only trout, that's about all we have in this high country. Never did any in the dead of winter though."

I said, "Hell Luke, we chop holes through two feet of ice in the winter to fish back in Minnesota."

Luke smiled at that, then he said, "Must want a fish pretty bad to work half a day just to find water to fish in. Bet you didn't go fishing too often." I laughed and explained that we opened several holes in different locations, but used them nearly every day. That way there was generally only an inch or so of surface ice to remove in the holes to go fishing again.

That night the pain in my back wouldn't let me sleep. The inside of my wound burned and throbbed. Luke washed the wound and put on clean bandages every few hours.

Luke said, "Tomorrow I'll search all the cabins and see if I can find anything to help us. I believe that wound's infected pretty good. The one damn thing I was afraid might happen."

By the next morning I was in bad shape. Luke got ready to leave and I asked him to get my journal and a pencil for me. He moved me under the window so I would have light to write by, stoked up the fire and left.

I knew I was slowly dying, and even if Luke found something

to help, it would be too late. My insides were on fire and I constantly drank water, only to sweat it back out. I owed Luke for what he had done for me. I had told him I would repay him and now I would do the only thing I could think of. I removed some pages from my journal and wrote to Luke. I wrote that I wanted him to go to Minnesota in the spring and find those people I had told him about over all those campfires. I wrote and drew him exact directions – what road numbers to look for – and even where he might find game to shoot. I also assured him of the welcome he would receive.

I then wrote a full page letter of introduction for him to give to Jenny and Jeb when he got there. In that letter I told Jenny and Jeb what kind of man they were meeting. A man to be trusted, a man who was my friend. The man who buried me.

I then drew a map for Luke to get to my little cabin from Island Lake. I wrote down what he should find there, fishing equipment, some clothes and even told him how to get to the little lake I fished, and where to find the hidden boat. Then, last of all, I entered in my journal that I was going to be buried here, on the slope to the lake near where the river entered it. I then wrote that I wanted Luke to read the entry on the inside cover that Jeb had written when I left Minnesota.

I closed it with, "I thank you Luke. Don't stay alone, it will slowly destroy what's left of your life. In the spring go to Minnesota and find what I should have never left."

Four days later, Luke stood near the lakeshore with head bowed over a rock covered grave. He was reading from a small black journal. He was reading the last lines:

"So stands a man. His
clearing around him, he
has no companions on the

hills. The lonely traveler,
looking up, wonders why he
was left when his companions
were taken."

When he finished, he realized why Dirk had wanted him to read it. It really wasn't for Dirk; it was for Luke, and he was now the lonely traveler that Dirk once was. He decided right then and there that he would do as Dirk asked. Come spring, he would head for northern Minnesota and find Dirk's people.

"Hell," he said to himself, "I might even chop me some holes through the ice and go fishin." He smiled down at the grave, figuring old Dirk would have got a chuckle out of that, turned and headed up the slope to the cabin.

Chapter 24

It was mid-June. The evening was cool and Jeb put another piece of wood on the fire. Jenny had just settled in her favorite chair after supper. It had been a long but rewarding day at the clinic. She had tended to a small boy who had cut himself on the leg trying to chop wood with a hatchet. She had just gotten comfortable in the chair when she thought she heard horses walking outside. Jeb, whose hearing was beginning to fail heard it a minute later, then lots of Indian children shouting in excitement.

The horses seemed to have stopped in front of their cabin. They both got up and walked out on the porch of the cabin. In front of the cabin stood two tired looking horses. On one horse there was a large pack with rifles tied to both sides. On the other horse sat a very tall, thin man. He had long blond hair, and a trimmed beard. He was dressed like a cowboy with a wide brimmed hat that covered the upper part of his face.

All the village children had gathered in a half circle behind the man. They stayed back with looks of wonderment and fear in their eyes. At least a dozen men from the village armed with rifles stood back amongst the trees and peered around the corners of neighboring cabins at the mounted tall stranger. They had not seen a horse in years. After the quakes, all the horses had been eaten.

It grew very quiet, then the man with a distinct western drawl said, "By chance would you folks be Jenny and Jeb?"

Jeb looked at Jenny, then turned to the man and said, "That's us, stranger, and who might you be?"

"Luke Bowdry's the name. I have a letter of introduction here from a mutual friend." He unbuttoned his coat and reached into his inside pocket for a tattered envelope that he held out for Jeb.

Jeb stepped down off the porch and took the envelope. When he did he couldn't help but notice the handle of a pistol protruding from under the man's left arm. He stepped back to the light from the open doorway, took out the letter and read:

> Dear Jenny and Jeb,
>
> I would like to introduce a man who I want you to welcome into your home as you would me. He is as good a man as you are ever going to meet. You can trust him completely, as I did. I've traveled great distances with him and lived with him. He respects people's rights and deals with violations of those rights in a just and swift manner.
>
> I have told him about you people and some of my past life that I spent with you. He comes to learn and you will learn from him.
>
> The best of luck to you all and I want you to know my last thoughts were of you.
>
> Yours forever,
>
> Dirk Volcots

"Step down Mr. Luke Bowdry, and welcome to our village and our humble home," Jeb said, as he turned and handed Jenny the letter. She took it with a questioning look and went into the cabin to read it.

Luke stepped down and started to tie the horses to the porch rail. He said as he looked at the circle of people around the yard, "Will my gear be alright if I leave it out here?"

Jeb smiled at him and said, "Nothing will be touched, would you like them watered?"

"That would be appreciated, I'll unpack them and stow it all here under cover on your porch."

Jeb called over one of the men and he led the two unpacked horses away. Jeb said, "Don't worry; that man used to raise horses before the quakes. They were all stolen by bandits and probably eaten in the end." He then led Luke into the cabin where Jenny was sitting by the fire with Dirk's letter in her lap.

She had been crying. She looked up and asked Luke, "So, Dirk is dead?"

"Yes ma'am, I'm sorry to say he is," Luke replied, "I understand he was real close to you folks."

Jenny said, "Yes, we thought a great deal of Dirk. Actually, I believe he saved us out on an island where we used to live in the summers. We shall miss him terribly. Perhaps sometime you can tell us how he came to die."

Then, showing her great strength, she rose and held out her hand to him. She said, "Luke, welcome to our home. You appear to have traveled a great distance. Please take a chair and I'll give you a nice plate of venison stew."

Luke shook her hand then took a seat at the table. In a few minutes she placed a large plate in front of him of the best stew he could remember eating. The first real potatoes he had seen in years – even wild onions and some things he had never tasted before, but were delicious.

He asked, "Where did you get potatoes?"

"Out of our village gardens," Jenny replied, "We grow lots of vegetables such as tomatoes, the onions you no doubt thought were wild, even rutabagas and beets. It's a village effort and everyone shares. Wild rice is really our mainstay and the harvesting in the fall is also a village effort. We do grow corn but due to not having any machinery to till the soil, we are limited as to space to grow things."

Luke said, "Don't problems ever arise with this sharing thing?"

Jenny said, "Oh yes, our system is not perfect but we have a village council that settles disputes. If the party involved doesn't agree to abide by the ruling of the council they must leave the village."

She went on. "One problem that has been growing is our supply of fresh meat, mainly venison. The hunters must travel long distances for game due to everything being killed or driven away near the village. They find ample game but transporting it back is the problem. Our hunters go out in two man parties and it's difficult for two men to carry an animal that weighs well over a hundred pounds for many miles."

"Jenny," Jeb said, "Perhaps a solution to that problem is now sitting at our table."

"You mean using my horses to haul in your game, don't you Jeb?" Luke said. "I might let them use Smokey, but no harm better come to him."

"Which one is Smokey?" Jenny asked.

Luke replied, "The big black. Dirk named him Smokey, and he was the horse he rode most of the time."

Jenny asked, "You mean you had other horses?"

"Yeah, I had two when Dirk and I met up in South Dakota. We picked up Smokey a couple of days later after a little altercation on the trail."

Jenny said, "You mean you took him from somebody."

"Yeah, you might say that, but then those fellas that had him didn't have any use for him anymore."

Jenny asked, "Why not? I wouldn't think any man would willingly give up a good horse in these times."

Luke simply said, "They were dead. They tried to hold me up for my horses and I killed them."

"Damn," Jeb said. "I believe fireside chats are going to get real interesting around here in the next few weeks. I can hardly wait to get started."

Jenny just shook her head, then she said to Luke, "You can bed down here in front of the fire. There in that lower cubbyhole you will find a mat to sleep on and some blankets. Jeb, you best get off to bed too. Luke is nearly asleep on his feet."

"She's right," Jeb said. "If you get cold, throw a chunk of wood on the fire. Jenny always has the coffee pot ready for the first person up and about to put on the stove in the morning. I'm sure that's going to be you. See you in the morning, Luke. Rest assured your horses and your gear won't be bothered." With that, Jeb headed for his bedroom.

As Jeb was leaving, Luke said, "One thing you need to understand, I'll loan you folks the use of Smokey, but if things don't work out here, both horses will leave with me."

"Understood," Jeb replied. "Now get some sleep. I have lots of things to show you tomorrow, including a pasture for your stock that may need a little fence mending."

Luke never did get out the fixings for his bed. He soon fell asleep in that big, soft chair. He was up at the crack of dawn. He had slept surprisingly well in that nice soft chair. He remembered to get a little fire going in the cook stove and put on the coffee. He then went out and walked the horses down to the lake to drink. He found a secluded place along the shore, stripped off his clothes and went for a swim. The water was cool and crystal clear. He loved to swim, but back home it was usually just small pools in the streams that he swam in.

When he got back to shore, the man who had tended to his horses the night before was standing there with a bundle of clothes in his arms. "Thought these might fit," he said. "If they do, you're welcome to them."

One thing Luke was short of was clothes. Being so tall and slim, most things he found in abandoned homes on the trail were either way too big or short in the legs. He tried on the pants and was surprised when they were a perfect fit. The shirt was a size too big but was in nice shape.

Luke said to the man, "Much obliged, and thanks for watering my stock last night. Luke Bowdry is my name," and extended his hand to the man.

"William Frey, just call me Bill," he said as he shook Luke's hand.

Luke said, "I'm told you're a horseman."

"Well, I used to keep a dozen head or so. Raised quarter horses mostly. I had a little success racing them down in the cities years ago. Used to be a nice track there called Canterbury Downs where they ran thoroughbreds and quarter horses. Did pretty well too. Then the quakes came and just like everything else in this old world, things went to hell. I tried to hang on to a few head, but in the end they weren't worth dying for."

Bill walked with Luke and the horses back to Jeb's cabin. Luke asked him if he knew about the pasture that Jeb had mentioned the night before and he said he knew where it was. He said it would work just fine and the boys in the village would be happy to haul water for the horses.

Luke smelled something cooking when he walked into the cabin. Jenny had breakfast ready, and Jeb was ready to show him around the village. When they got to the pasture, Jeb had mentioned they were surprised to find the repair work was well under way. Bill had a crew of the older boys and a few of the men cutting birch poles to fill in places where the old fence wire was gone. By late afternoon the two horses were in their new home. There was a small tank for water that was supplied happily as Bill had said, by the village boys. They didn't have to haul it far because the lake was just across the road from the pasture.

Luke couldn't help but notice Bill's oldest son, a boy of about fifteen, stayed close to the horses. He had come up with a brush and was working on Smokey. Luke picked up his short lead rope and walked out to them. He tied the lead rope to both sides of the rope halter on Smokey and threw the loop back over his head for a rough set of reins. He said to the boy, "Take him for a ride before dark. You and your dad are in charge of these two when I ain't around."

Luke had made sure that the other boys heard him when he said who was in charge. The boy's face lit up and he jumped on the horse. Luke knew he had made a good decision. The next day a hunting party went out, and the boy on Smokey went along.

Chapter 25

In the weeks that followed, Luke learned things from morning to night. His diet changed completely from nearly all meat every day to boiled dinners, rice dishes and a few things he wasn't sure of, but were mighty tasty. He even grew to like the coffee, or what was called coffee that was actually a kind of wild tea.

Jeb taught him how to fish for walleye and northern pike. As Dirk had done in the past, he did the rowing while Jeb did most of the fishing. Each hour in that boat was like attending classes in geophysics. He learned a lot from Jeb about what caused earthquakes and volcanic eruptions. It seemed like the man could talk on the subject forever, but it was interesting.

Not only was the man an expert of seismic activity, he was also one hell of a fisherman. He showed Luke how to dry meat and smoke fish. He told him about how they gathered maple syrup in the early spring and harvested wild rice in the fall. Also, there were evening fireside chats that Jenny joined in on. She shared her wealth of knowledge on healing with herbs. She knew all about what plants were edible and their food value. Also, her knowledge of Indian history was fascinating.

When Luke wasn't fishing with Jeb he would go out with a hunting party. It wasn't long before he gained considerable respect among the hunters for being a crack shot. In return, he learned the Ojibwa were very skilled in locating and tracking game. They seemed to see tracks he couldn't see. It was like they had a sixth sense when it came to hunting.

The Indians greatly appreciated using the horse to carry game back to the village. The horse also carried their gear to the area they were going to hunt. Luke found the Indians took good care of his horses and when he went to check on them he always found their water tank filled with fresh water.

As the summer passed, he began to think about visiting Dirk's cabin. He had talked about it to several of the village Indians and they had seen it when they hunted in that area. They preferred to sleep in the woods when they were out hunting unless the weather was bad so none of them had used the cabin. They did say it appeared to still be in good repair and livable.

Luke, not being used to being around people, developed a need for a little solitude. He brought it up one day when fishing with Jeb. Jeb understood how he could have such a feeling, having been alone for several years. He told Luke that now would be a good time to go. Wild rice harvesting would be starting in a few weeks and as he had told him before, all the village people worked together to bring in the harvest.

That night as they sat by the fire, Luke showed him the map that Dirk had given him. Jeb assured him the map was excellent and he would have no problem finding the cabin. He suggested that Luke travel by foot because the road was impassable and he would have to wade through several swamps.

Luke agreed and the next morning he walked over to Bill's cabin and told him he would be leaving for a couple of weeks and wouldn't be taking his horses. Bill agreed to look after the animals. With that taken care of, Luke started to prepare a backpack for the trip. He planned to leave the following morning.

Jenny put so many items in the pack that Luke was beginning to wonder if he would be able to carry it. He tried to cut back on some of the things, but she overruled him. He sure wasn't used to being fussed over by a woman.

Jeb even got in on it. He told her, "Good God woman, you're going to put the man's back out carrying all that weight. He's coming back in a couple of weeks. If he eats all the stuff in that pack he won't be in shape to make the journey back here." Before going to bed that night, Jeb asked him, "Would you like a book to take with you? I recall Dirk liked to bring along a little something to read when he went back to his cabin every now and then."

That made Luke recall something Dirk had talked about. He said, "Dirk mentioned a book you had written or were writing when he left to go west. Did you ever finish it?"

"Why yes, I did," Jeb replied. "I finished it and made a school project of making copies. The history of this settlement and our survival is in that book."

He got up and walked over to a bookshelf. He picked one out and handed it to Luke. "Take it along. Let me know what you think of it when you return. You will find Dirk is a big part of that book and our history here. It tells how he had to take human life and how he saved us from an evil man."

Two days later Luke found Dirk's cabin and settled in. The cabin was still in good shape and he could almost feel Dirk's presence. After eating, he sat in the doorway of the cabin thinking about how his life had changed. For the first time in years, he had people that he could trust that seemed to care about him. People he could call his friends. Thanks to the chance meeting of a walking man headed west through South Dakota, he had a whole new life to look forward to. It saddened him that the man wasn't there to share the life with him.

As he watched the sun settle into the tall birches to the west, a feeling of peace settled over him. A feeling he had almost forgotten could exist. He would occasionally return to this place. He would use it as a kind of retreat. A place to remember the past in the peace and quiet, and think of what might have been.

As the darkness descended he entered the cabin and lit some of the candles Jenny had provided. Searching through his pack he found the book Jeb had sent along. He settled down at the table and started to read.

The first few chapters were mostly about Jeb, Jenny, and Jenny's husband Calvin. They told of their struggle to survive in the new world. Reading it brought back memories of his own hardships. The loss of his ranch and his beloved family. As he turned the page to the next chapter, he heard the long, mournful howl of a timber wolf off in the distance. It seemed somehow appropriate because the next chapter of the book was titled: *Dirk and the Bar-Track Man.*